Louis L'amour

The Shadow Riders

CORGI BOOKS

THE SHADOW RIDERS
A CORGI BOOK 0 552 12154 1

First publication in Great Britain

PRINTING HISTORY
Corgi edition published 1983

Copyright © 1982 by Louis L'amour Enterprises, Inc.
Front cover copyright © 1982 by Lou Glanzman

This book is set in Baskerville

Corgi Books are published by
Transworld Publishers Ltd.,
Century House, 61–63 Uxbridge Road,
Ealing, London W5 5SA

Printed and bound in Great Britain by
Cox & Wyman Ltd, Reading

To the cast and crew of
The Shadow Riders

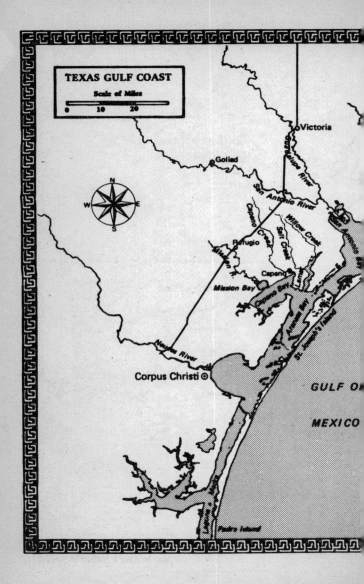

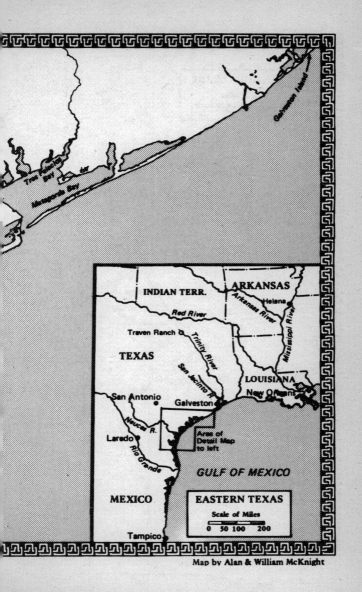

Map by Alan & William McKnight

The Shadow Riders

ONE

Hunching his shoulders against the cold, pelting rain, Major Mac Traven slipped a hand under his caped coat to assure himself his spare pistol remained in position. A sudden gust of wind rattled rain upon his campaign hat and spattered his face and hands.

Desperately tired and carrying the gnawing hunger from three missed meals, he glanced back along the road at the scattered travellers.

They were an army no longer; like himself they were just tired men returning to homes left long ago. Once they had marched with the proud steps of men with a mission to be accomplished; now they plodded wearily, heads down against the rain, thinking only of home.

Under the bare black trees water gathered in pools like mirrors of steel as the rain fell from the sullen sky. Somewhere ahead was a town, if such it could be called, a dismal place by all accounts, but it held the promise

1

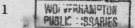

of a hot meal and grain for his horse. More he could not expect, yet there might be a letter.

"Watch yourself," he had been warned. "All but the Swede are a pack of thieves. They will steal anything they can put their hands on and murder you if need be."

It was late afternoon when Mac rode into the town's one street, a muddy, rutted alleyway between two rows of nondescript shacks, sodden with rain. Dimly, at the end of the street and through a veil of rain, he glimpsed the river and a steamboat landing.

Here and there a horse was tied to hitching-rails or awning posts. Some of the horses he recognized as those of other soldiers returning from the War.

He turned aside at the log barn that had been described to him and rode around it to the wide open door and the pole corral. He was stepping down from the saddle when a big man with yellow hair appeared in the barn door.

"Olson?"

"Come." The big man motioned him into the barn. "Who told you of me?"

"A steamboat pilot at Helena, on the Mississippi. He said you were the only honest man in town."

The big Swede did not smile. "There is one other," he spoke with only a slight accent. "How long you stay?"

"Over-night."

"Two-bits, then. You can sleep in the hay."

"Isn't there somewhere I can find a bed?"

"A bed with bugs, yes. A bed where you will be robbed. It is no good, those beds."

"I was told there might be mail?"

Mac Traven was as tall as the Swede, although not as

heavy. He led his horse to a stall and forked some hay into the manger.

Olson indicated a building. "At the store there is a box. Sometimes there is mail."

"A friend knew I'd be coming this way," Mac said. "It's been four years since I heard from my family." He wiped the rain from his face with a handkerchief. "They live in Texas, and I guess to them I chose the wrong side."

Leaving the stable he walked across the muddy street. Going up the steps he paused to stomp the mud from his boots. Inside the store the air was hot and close. Several men sat or stood around a pot-bellied stove, and a man behind the counter in undershirt and suspenders came over to him. "What's fer y'?"

"Is there any mail for Mac Traven?"

The man behind the counter indicated a box. "If so, it'll be there. You take a look."

A man who had come into the store behind him took the pipe from his mouth. "Traven, did you say? You got any kin in these parts?"

"Not that I know of."

"There's a Johnny Reb down in the shack by the boat landing. Wounded man. They're fixin' to hang him. Kangaroo court."

He had his hand in the mail-box, and now he swiftly withdrew it. He wheeled and ran for the door. Chances are it was somebody else, but—!

Going out the door he heard someone say, "There's a man fixin' to git killed!"

He glimpsed the roof of the shack through the trees near the landing and went down the muddy slope on the run, unbuttoning his coat as he went.

The trouble was there, right in front of him, as he entered the room. Two men held the arms of a dark, handsome young man who had been shot and was badly in need of a shave. Another man was putting a noose over his head. The other end of the rope had been thrown over a rafter and was held by three other men.

All eyes turned toward him as Traven stepped through the door, gun in hand. "Let him go," he said.

There were six of them in all, rough, dirty, and bearded men born to trouble and bad whiskey. "Who the Hell d' you think you are, comin' in here an' tellin' us what to do?"

Another of the men spoke contemptuously. "Sorry, Mister Major, them braids don't count for nothin' no more. The War's over."

"I said to let him go."

"Now, you see here, Major! We got us a Reb, an' he's goin' to git hung. If you don't want to watch, you jus' git goin'. I say hangin's too good for Rebs!"

"You just said the War was over. Mr. Lincoln said the same thing. Take the rope off him."

"Lincoln don't count for much here. We can handle our own Rebs, an' no politician is goin' to tell us how. Nor no Army major, either!"

A stocky, red-haired man interrupted. "Maybe we should hang the two of them. Make us a nice brace of chickens!"

Mac Traven tilted his pistol. "Take the rope off him. Take it off *now!*"

They hesitated a moment; then carefully, the rope was lifted off. As they let go of their prisoner he started to fall, and Mac stepped forward quickly, catching him around the body with his left arm. As he did so, one of the men threw a rifle to his shoulder, and Traven fired.

The bullet caught the man in mid-movement. He stopped, started to speak, then fell head-long.

The others backed off, and Mac Traven spoke quietly, almost indifferently. "If you boys are counting, I've got four cartridges left in the gun, and there's five of you here. As you've noticed, I hit what I shoot at. That means one of you might live." He smiled a beautiful smile with even white teeth. "Who wants to be the lucky man?"

"Ain't worth it," the red-head replied. "But what're you doin', a Union officer stickin' up for a Johnny Reb?"

"Like you said, the War's over, and he's not a Johnny Reb any longer. But I've a better reason. He's my brother."

Without taking his eyes from the others he said, "Dal? You've got to walk. We're gettin' out of here."

"Duff . . ." Dal Traven muttered. "Duffle."

Mac gestured with the gun barrel. "You! All of you! Back against the wall!"

They moved, some quickly, others more slowly. On a pallet near the far wall he saw a duffle-bag and a haversack. He helped Dal to the door, then walked back for his gear.

"You'll get no more trouble from us," the red-head said, "but that man you killed has friends."

"He bought his ticket," Mac Traven said, "and I've got more rides on the same train."

"You're pretty handy with that gun. You one o' them Texians?"

"You could say that." Helping Dal, he eased out of the door and closed it behind him. Under the trees he stopped and lowered the gear to the ground.

"Have you got a horse, Dal?"

"I've got Bonnie Prince." Weak as he was, Dal could still hold a gun, and Mac passed him the pistol. "He's yonder in the stable. That's why they were hangin' me. They wanted my gear, my rifle, and my horse. That Johnny Reb thing was just an excuse."

"Can you keep them inside?"

"I'll try, Mac. I'm weak, but I can still shoot."

There were several horses in the barn, but he had no trouble remembering Bonnie Prince, a horse he had helped to raise. Saddling up, he listened for trouble. Dal was obviously in bad shape, but he knew his brother would ride until he fell from the saddle.

Olson opened the barn door as Mac approached. "Is it you who shoots?"

"I'll need my horse, Olson."

"You get him. I get you some grub."

Olson went into the tack room where he was living while Mac saddled the gray. "Sorry, old boy," he apologized. "I meant for you to have some rest."

Mac rode his horse outside and helped Dal into the saddle. Olson walked over and held up a sack and a coffee-pot tied to it. "There is grub and coffee. You ride now."

"Olson, there has to be a special place in Valhalla for men like you." He gripped the Swede's hand. "If you come to Texas there's always a place at the table for you."

"Maybe I come soon."

"Come when you will, Olson. There's good farm-land further west where a man like you could make it pay. Get you away from this river riff-raff."

"Aye, I t'ink I come."

With a fast mile behind them, Mac slowed the pace. "Can you make it, Dal?"

"I've been thrown off, Mac, but I never fell off. You just keep a-goin'. All I want is to get home. I want to see the folks again. I want to put my feet under ma's table. I just want to *be* there!"

"Me, too, Dal. Let's go."

They walked their horses into the night, but Mac

knew they could not go far. The big gray was a splendid horse, but he was used up. They would have to find a place to rest and hide.

They rode past rail fences and muddy lanes, old log barns and patches of forest. In the distance, they saw a lighted window. "Somebody sick," Mac commented. At that hour there'd be no reason for a farmer to be up. They remembered such times from their own home.

"You heard from the folks?" Mac asked.

"They think I'm dead."

"How's that?"

"My outfit was cut off, almost wiped out. Took us six weeks, travellin' by night to get back to our own people. I'd been reported killed in action."

"I had no mail," Mac said. "There wasn't much chance, south to north."

Behind some woods he found an old log barn. Inside it was dry and clean, smelling of new-mown hay, although at this time of year that was unlikely. Tying their horses in two of the stalls, Mac put hay into the mangers, and scrounging around, found some corn in a bin, which he also gave the horses.

Dal had stretched out in the hay and was asleep almost at once.

Mac Traven went to the door and peered outside. It was still raining, but risk or no risk, Dal must have rest, and so must their horses. All was quiet but the falling rain. He waited at the door, listening, then walked back and lay down in the hay.

Four years . . . he was just past thirty and pa would be pushing sixty-five, and ma was a good ten years younger. He was a poor hand at remembering ages and

had only the vaguest idea of how old his sister was.
Girls changed so fast once they started to grow up.

When the War broke out he fled Texas in the night,
determined to fight to preserve the Union. He felt, as
old Sam Houston had, that their first loyalty was to the
nation. Dal had felt otherwise and joined a Texas cavalry outfit.

Mac lay back on the hay, hands clasped behind his
head, ears tuned for the slightest sound. The sound of
rain on the roof was pleasant and he was very tired, yet
if he slept their enemies might come upon them unheard.

Before the War he had served four years with the
Texas Rangers, four years of almost continual warfare
with Comanches, Kiowas, and border bandits. Upon his
arrival in Ohio his skills were discovered, and among
men who knew nothing of actual combat his advance-
ment was rapid.

At last, he was going home. Four years as a Ranger
and now four years in the Army with no visits at all.

It was he who had located their original ranch, seeing
it first when on patrol with the Rangers, and buying it
from old Sandoval, who wanted to live his last years in
San Antonio. Twenty-three thousand acres of Spanish
land grant. Then he had ridden alone into Comanche
country to see old Rising Water.

The old Comanche had studied him shrewdly as they
sat cross-legged in his lodge, knowing all the while who
he was and that he had been a Ranger. "Are you a
friend to the Comanche?" Rising Water had asked.

"I have fought the Comanche and found them great
warriors. I was honored by their courage. If the
Comanche come to me in peace, there shall be peace
between us. If they come to me in war, who am I to
refuse them?"

Mac indicated things he placed upon the ground. "I

have bought this land from Sandoval. In addition I would give this to you who are Comanches. Twenty new skinning knives, twenty new blankets, three sacks of sugar, and five fat steers, and there shall be five fat steers each year for five years. . . ."

Suddenly Dal's voice interrupted his thoughts. "Mac? It was bushwhackers tried to kill me. It was them who wounded me and left me for dead, and they knew me, Mac, they knew who they were shooting at."

Mac waited, listening. They *knew* Dal? What could that mean?

"I heard them, Mac. One of them said, 'that's Dal Traven. That's one more of them we don't have to worry about.' "

Mac raised up on one elbow. "Are you sure? This is a long way from Texas."

"I'm sure. The man who shot me was riding Ranch Baby."

Ranch Baby? Pa's sorrel gelding, the colt born shortly after they moved on the place.

Suddenly, Mac was scared. Had something gone wrong back home? Or was it simply a case of a stolen horse?

No . . . everything would be all right. Pa was there, and Jesse. Jesse would be a man now.

TWO

When morning showed its light through the cracks in the barn door, Mac Traven brushed the hay and straw away from a place on the dirt floor and built a fire there. Then he got out the Swede's coffee-pot and made coffee. There was a chunk of bread in the pack and some dried beef and venison.

Dal opened his eyes to the fire and lay quiet, looking at it and feeling better than he had in weeks.

"Coffee smells good," he said, "and there's warmth in the fire."

"That's stored-up sunlight, boy," Mac said, smiling. "Through all its long years that tree was catching sunlight and storin' it away for this moment. What you see in that fire is something captured from the sun."

Carefully, Dal sat up, reaching for his boots. "I remember the fires back home when you or pa started them up of a morning. I never enjoyed them quite as

10

much after I had to do the starting myself. I used to scrunch down in my blankets until the fire warmed up the room.

"I remember how we used to stand at the loop-holes peekin' out to see if there was Injun sign before we opened the door. And then we'd stand waitin' a bit and watchin' color come into the sky.

"Ol' Tennessee hound would scout the barn and corrals for us, and if there was an Injun around he'd let us know soon enough.

"By that time ma would have some bacon on, if we had any, or beef if we hadn't, an' by the time we got back to the house our breakfast was on an' ready. Man, I've thought of those breakfasts many a time durin' this war."

Mac saddled their horses and then returned to the fire for bread and jerked beef. They sat in silence, chewing, and then Mac said, "At least you've Kate to wait for you."

"She's waitin', I guess. We sort of taken it for granted, the two of us. I don't recall ever sayin' much about it, but we had it in mind."

"You've got to ask them, Dal. Women like to be asked. It never pays to take anything for granted."

They drank the last of the coffee, and Mac put out the fire, covering it with dirt from the floor. Then he offered a hand to Dal.

Dal said, "You mount up. I'm not as fit as I might be, but I can still climb into a saddle." Dal put a foot in the stirrup, hesitated, and then heaved himself into the saddle, but when he sat solid with his feet in the stirrups his face was white and sick.

Mac said, "As long as you're up there, you ride out first, but keep your rifle handy. I'll close the door behind us. Somebody else might need a dry place to sleep."

Mac Traven led the way, avoiding the road and trouble that might be waiting. If the man he'd killed had kin-folk they might be scouting the country by now. He led the way down a wooded lane where two wagon tracks were, and around the base of a hill and across a field into a stone-dotted pasture where thin grass grew over the roll of the hills. There were patches of black-jack brush and occasionally a cow.

By the time the noon sun was high they had a winding twelve miles behind them, and Mac was breathing easier. He glanced back at Dal, who was slumping in the saddle, riding more from instinct than knowledge of what he was about. Ahead there was a place where the trail dipped down into trees, and Mac could see the sparkle of running water.

It was almighty still, and there was nobody around a body could see. Mac helped Dal from the saddle and let him lie on the grass. "I'm sorry," Dal muttered, "right sorry."

Mac watered the horses and let them graze on the grass near the stream, then carried water to Dal, handing him a twist of jerky as he did so.

"We won't chance a fire and the smell of smoke," he said. "Have yourself some of this jerky and chew it well. Make it last, is what I mean. We've a long ride ahead of us."

"You holdin' anything? I mean, have you got money?"

"Mighty little," Mac said. "When we get along further we might shoot something to eat. Or maybe we can come up to some farm house where the woman of the place would feed us."

"You was always good at that," Dal said wryly. "Every

woman you ever met wanted to feed you an' do for you."

"Sometimes I was lucky," Mac agreed, with a smile, "but you don't always find them when you need them."

When the horses were rested they mounted up and followed a muddy lane back to the main trail. Mac looked both ways and took off his coat and tied it behind the saddle. With his coat off Dal saw the tube slung from Mac's right shoulder and buckled to his belt so it wouldn't move around when he rode.

"What's that?" Dal wondered aloud.

"A Blakeslee Quick-Loader for my Spencer rifle. The Spencer carries seven shots, eight if you have one in the chamber. This Quick-Loader has tubes in it of seven cartridges each. They come in different sizes— seven, ten, and thirteen. I hear they made some that carried six tubes, too, but I never saw one. This one of mine has thirteen tubes."

"I'll be damned! When your rifle's empty you just shove in another tube?"

"That's right. We were trained to load 'em so we could maintain a fire of fourteen to fifteen shots a minute."

For three days they rode west and south, for three days each daybreak found them in the saddle, and for three days they saw no house and no trail and only occasionally crossed pony trails or the marks of wagon wheels.

By the fourth day Dal was building the fire, gathering fuel for it, and moving around, taking his time.

"Be good to be home," he said, looking off to the south, where the grass ran into the horizon.

"Pa will be getting along," Mac said. "He'll need help runnin' the place. Of course, Jesse's there."

"Maybe not," Dal said. "He was talkin' of war himself. You know how it is. When everybody else is going, he would want to go, too."

Mac turned in his saddle and glanced back along the trail. If anyone was following him because of the man he killed, by staying off the trail he might have avoided them. It did not pay to take an enemy lightly.

In any event there was much potential danger. During the War a lot of renegades had hung about the fringes of the War, using it as an excuse for looting, stealing stock, and brutalizing unprotected citizens. Now those renegades would be along the roads, robbing whomever they could.

The country was facing a difficult period of readjustment. With the War ended the men from the South would be returning home to a largely devastated land. The slaves on whom they depended for labor would be gone, and they would have no money to hire labor. There would be a shortage of food, a shortage of farm stock, and a lack of capital with which to restock and rebuild.

In the north the situation would be scarcely better, as munition plants would be closing down. Textile manufacturers would no longer have an army to clothe, and a lot of people were going to be out of work.

"We're lucky, Dal," Mac said. "We've got the ranch to go to. There will at least be beef to eat, and we can start building back. Texas didn't suffer much from the War, and with all of us working it shouldn't take long."

"Kate will be there," Dal said. "I never knew I could miss anybody so much."

Mac glanced back again. Four Confederate soldiers had come into sight, one man riding, three walking, probably taking turns with the horse. Ahead and on the right there was a farm. Smoke rose from the chimney, but the corral was empty.

Dal was looking better as they got further away from the low country near the river. The air was better, and if nothing happened to change things he would be himself again.

Mac thought about Kate. Kate was quite a woman, although she and Dal had never actually become engaged. If Dal had been reported dead, what would she do? Wait a decent interval and find herself another man. Had Dal considered that?

The trail ahead dipped into woods along the creek. Mac Traven carried two pistols, the one in his holster and a spare in his waist-band, but it was the Spencer he preferred. Army issue was .52 calibre, and it packed a wallop. He slid the Spencer from the saddle scabbard and held it in his hands as they rode into the woods.

They were seeing fewer soldiers now. This was Indian country, and those Indians who had fought on one side or the other lived further east.

On the next morning Mac killed a deer in the river bottom, and they held up a day to smoke the meat, eating venison steaks while waiting for the smoke to do its job. "We're gettin' close," Dal said. "I remember the time we rode north a buffalo huntin' an' camped by this same stream."

"If we're lucky we'll make it some time tomorrow."

Yet when afternoon came great thunderheads were piling up in the sky ahead of them, and they could hear a distant rumble of thunder.

"Rain," Dal said irritably. "We could do without that!"

Mac pushed on ahead. Unless they got under cover in a hurry they were in for a soaking. He topped out on a low rise and saw a roof-top ahead and off to one side of the dim track they were following.

The clouds were over-head now, and he could see a

broadening white streak along the horizon. When that reached them it would be raining. "Come on!" he yelled and charged down the slope, Dal following.

There was a corral with the gate-bars down, the corral empty. There was a small barn and a log cabin. No smoke came from the chimney, but there was a stack of cut wood against the near wall of the cabin.

No tracks led into the place, which only meant nobody had been there since the last rain. He swung down. "Dal? You take the horses while I scout the cabin."

Dal caught the reins of Mac's horse and started toward the barn.

Mac hesitated, then rapped on the door. The sound echoed hollowly, but there was no response. He tried the door, and it gave under his hand. He stepped inside. "Anybody home?" he asked, but the room was empty.

A fire-place, a bed, a bench, and one chair. Cooking pans, polished and clean but dust covered, hung in place. There was a table covered with oil-cloth and the remains of a candle that had burned down to only a pool of melted wax, and little of that except what had dripped down to the mantle.

There was a door to another room, covered with a hanging blanket. He looked around again, listening for Dal.

Somebody had been living here. He looked again at the curtain and spoke aloud again. "Anybody home?"

There was a roll of thunder, closer now, and he heard running feet outside. Then the door burst open. It was Dal. He ducked inside just as the rain came, and it came with a thundering roar.

Dal glanced around, then he glanced at the blanket-curtain. "You been in there?"

"No . . . not yet. What's in the barn?"

"Three head of good horses, half starved. I forked some hay for them."

Reluctantly, Mac crossed to the blanket, gathered the edge as Dal drew a pistol.

Abruptly, he drew back the blanket.

There was a window at the side, and there was a bed, a chair, and a large chest for storing clothes. And in the bed there was a child . . . a girl.

She was sitting up in bed, clutching a rag doll. Her hair was touseled and blond.

"Hello! Are you my Daddy?"

THREE

Mac Traven was startled. "Me? No, missy, I'm afraid not. Don't you know your own father?"

"No, sir. He went away to war when I was small. Mama said he would be coming back soon. She said the War was over now."

"She was surely right about that. Where is your mama?"

"She's gone. Some bad men came and took her away. I didn't think they were bad men at first because they wore those gray uniforms," she pointed at Dal, "like he does. But they took mama away. They dragged her."

"And they just left you here? Alone?"

"Mama didn't tell them about me. I don't think she did. She was afraid, and I think she knew they were coming, because when she came in she was all scared and everything. She said some bad men were taking women away and that if they came here

18

I should keep very still and wait, that papa would come."

"How've you been getting along?" Dal asked. "Have you been eating?"

"Oh, yes! There's milk. There's some left, anyway. And there's cheese mama made, and bread she baked for papa."

"How long have you been here alone?"

"See?" she pointed at a calendar. "I scratch off the days. It is four days."

Dal looked around. "Snug cabin." He glanced at the little girl. "Is it all right if we stay here tonight? We're going home."

"You can stay. I wish you would. At night sometimes it is scary. I think about wolves an' Indians an' ghosts an' such."

"What's your name, honey?" Mac asked.

"I'm Susan. I am Susan Atherton."

Dal glanced at Mac, then at her. "*Jim* Atherton?"

"Yes. Did you know him?"

Dal's face was pale and he turned toward the fire-place. "I knew him in passing, sort of. I mean I never knew him well."

Dal started for the door. "I'll fetch some wood. Mac? You want to help me?"

Outside, Dal said, "Mac? We've got to take her with us. We'll have to take her home. Jim Atherton's dead. He was killed by a sharpshooter, last day of the War."

"What about this business? Men in gray uniforms carrying off women? That doesn't seem like any Southerners we know."

"There's all kinds." Dal thought a moment. "Could be Colonel Ashford. He was headed this way, but I didn't think he'd bother women-folks. Always seemed a gentleman." He paused. "He wanted me to come with him and keep on fightin'. The War may be over for you an' me but it ain't over for Ashford. When Lee surrendered he was fit to be tied. Called him a traitor, a coward, whatever he could think of."

"We'd better go back inside. She'll be afraid we left her, too."

"Damn it, Mac! What's got into the man? Draggin' women-folks away to God knows what?"

"Dal? There's women-folks at our place, too. And it can't be more'n thirty-five, forty miles from here."

"I was thinkin' of that. No use to start now. We'd kill our horses before we made it. Let 'em rest, eat, an' we'll ride out in the mornin'."

Mac went back through the door and watched the girl, finally saying, "Susan? I think when we leave in the morning we'd better take you with us. Your papa may be some time in getting here, and we'll leave a note for him. We've got some folks down south of here, and you can stay with them."

She looked at them, round-eyed and serious. "Mama said I was to wait for papa."

Mac squatted down beside her. "Susan, the War is over, but it may take some time for all the soldiers to come home. We don't know where your papa was, and he might have to walk all the way from Pennsylvania or Virginia. You had better come and stay with us until he can come for you."

In a cyclone cellar near the house they found several slabs of bacon hanging, a half barrel of potatoes, and one of carrots and onions. Some of the potatoes had begun to sprout. The milk was kept in a cool place, a small pit slabbed with rock. The milk was beginning to turn, but there was butter-milk and a little cheese.

"Your mother must have been a worker," Dal commented as Mac put food on the table.

"I helped. I can work, too."

"How old are you, Susan?"

"I am eight years old. I helped mama with everything. I can milk a cow, and I can churn butter, and I helped dig the vegetables."

She ate in silence for a few minutes and then asked, "Do you have little girls where you live?"

"Well, we have girls. We have sisters, and one of them wasn't much older than you when we left, but that was four years ago."

After they had eaten, Mac put a hand on her shoulder. "Susan, you go along to bed now, and don't you worry about those things that go bump in the night. We'll be here."

When she was gone they sat at the table drinking coffee, occasionally feeding the fire. "What about Ashford?" Mac asked.

"Tough man, good soldier, and he always seemed a good man, but war changes people. He recruited a lot of bad ones to keep his strength up, and toward the end he was letting them act like bandits just to keep them with him. To be honest about it, some of the officers were beginning to avoid him, and when Lee surrendered Ashford took it almost as a personal insult. The last I heard he was headed for Mexico."

It was bleak and cold when morning came and they saddled up, adding several slabs of bacon and some vegetables to their packs.

"We'll take one horse with us an' turn the others loose," Mac said. "There's plenty of grass, and there's a creek down yonder. They'll make out."

Susan came to the kitchen, dressed for travel. She had made a small bundle of her clothes, and she stood waiting, her sun-bonnet in her hand. For a moment she stood silent in the door to her room, watching them.

"Better have something to eat," Dal said. "It is a long ride."

"All right. I'm not very hungry."

At the last, when Dal helped her into the saddle she said, "What if mama comes back?"

"We left a note," Mac said, "and people hereabouts are kindly toward the homes of others. Sometimes travellers sleep in them, but they always leave them clean and with fuel ready for the fire."

At the crest of a low hill Susan turned for one look back, but when they had ridden several miles and stopped atop another hill to give the horses a breather, she said, "You don't think papa is coming back, do you?"

Dal tried to speak, swallowed a couple of times, and put a hand on her shoulder. "I'm afraid not, Susan. War is a hard time for all of us. There will be a lot who never get back."

"Is papa gone, then?"

"Yes, honey, I'm afraid he is. I knew Jim Atherton. He was a good man. We soldiered together."

"Mama woke up one night, crying. I think she knew. I think she felt he was gone. She did not say it, but she told me we might have to go away."

Dal glanced at Mac and they rode on, keeping Susan between them as they rode single file.

The country was wide open and empty, with scattered clumps of trees on hillsides or along the ridges. Every stream was lined with trees. It was almost noon when Mac Traven pulled up sharply.

"Dal? Look here . . ."

Dal rode up, and Mac indicated the trail he had just cut. It had been made by a large party of horsemen driving some cattle and with one wagon, heavily loaded.

"Dozen at least, maybe twenty or more. Shod horses,

headin' right down our way. It could be them, Mac. We'd better hurry."

"Sundown at the earliest, and when we come up on the place we'd better ride careful."

"Is it the men who took mama?"

"Could be, Susan. If we run into trouble you drop off that horse and lie flat, d' you hear?"

Mac Traven scouted back along the trail, then returned. "We'll find a camp somewhere ahead. No use wastin' time studying the back trail."

"That trail's three, maybe four days old."

"It is. But if we can find a camp we can get a better idea of how many there are and who they have with them."

Dal glanced at the sky. "Looks like rain. That'll slow 'em up."

"But not much. They've been stealin' women, and somebody will know and will start hunting them."

Here and there they could pick out a distinctive horse-track, one that would help in the future. "Wonder they didn't loot the house and find Susan, here."

"Mama was away from the house, looking for our cow. They looked at the house, but they didn't come near."

"Didn't want to chance it," Dal suggested. "They had the woman, and there might be a man with a rifle at the house."

They stopped only briefly at mid-day to rest the horses and let them graze. Dal paced impatiently, swearing under his breath. Mac lay on his back, his hat over his eyes. "Take it easy, Dal. Save your strength. We'll need all we got when we come up to them."

"If we do. This here may be a long chase."

"Maybe. But pa was at home, and Jesse. You know Jesse. He was always good with a gun."

"If he was there. And if pa was there. They might have been out on the range lookin' after stock, and these people don't waste around. You saw that back there."

Through the long, still afternoon they followed the trail, approaching every patch of brush with care, riding slowly up each slope to see over it without being seen. "Headin' right for our place," Dal said once, "almost as if they knew it was there."

"Maybe one of them does," Mac said. "Somebody knows the country, looks like to me."

"Let's study on that," Dal suggested. "Maybe we can figure their next camp."

"Hell," Mac said, "we know where that'll be. We've got the best water in the country around. They will stop at our place."

A few spattering drops of rain fell, and Dal held back, helping Susan with her slicker. It was one that had belonged to her father and covered her like a tent. "Room for two of you in there," he said, smiling. "You holdin' up all right?"

"Yes, sir. I used to ride to town with mama, and that was thirty miles."

"Let's go then."

Mac had ridden on ahead, but now he had reined in and was waiting. "Look at this." He pointed at a fresh lot of tracks.

The tracks were of five riders in a bunch, driving several head of cattle.

"Foragers, rounding up everything they can," Dal said. "We'd best ride careful. We might come up on some of them."

"Ain't heard any shooting," Mac added.

The rain fell softly, but the trail ahead was broad and

easy to follow. At each rise they walked their horses until they could peer over, then rode on.

"How far would you say?" Dal asked.

"Five, six miles."

"Let's swing off to the west and come up that draw behind the barn. Give us a little cover until we're right close."

They drew up when they reached the draw, listening. There was no sound but the rain.

"Susan," Dal said gently, "if you see your ma, don't you yell out. There'll be maybe twenty of them and only two of us. We may have to back off and wait until night-time."

"I used to go hunting with papa. I can be quiet."

"Good girl. Mac, it looks like we picked a winner when we tied up with Susan."

A trickle of water ran down the draw. The air was very still, the clouds low. Their horses' hoofs made almost no sound on the wet grass. Twice more they drew up to listen, but there was no sound.

Suddenly, Mac drew up, pointing.

A dead and butchered steer lay on the ground near some bushes. The best cuts of meat had been taken, the rest abandoned to the coyotes, which had already been at it.

"At least two days. Maybe three. I think they've come and gone."

"Careful, then, when we ride up. Pa always could shoot."

Over the edge of the draw they could see the roof and the chimney. There was no smoke. Nor was there any sound. Suddenly, Dal put spurs to his horse. "To Hell with it!" he said, and pistol in hand he charged up the bank of the draw and into the empty yard.

He pulled up sharply. The corral bars were down,

and the door hung on its hinges, gaping wide. He swung down and ran into the house.

Mac faced the barn. That door was open also, but there was no sign of life. Rifle up, he walked his horse toward the corral, then drew up.

Old Shep lay there, bloody and dead, a bit of cloth still gripped in his teeth. It was a bloody cloth. Mac swore and turned away. Susan looked at him, wide-eyed and sad.

"He was your dog?"

"He was our dog. We all owned him, we all loved him. He'd been with us since I was a youngster, seems like."

Dal came out of the house. "They've been here. No sign of pa, ma, or Gretchen. Jesse was here. His bed's been slept in. They must have taken him, too."

Slowly, Mac dismounted and helped Susan to the ground. "No use killin' our horses. We've a long ride ahead of us. Let's fix some grub."

"You fix it," Dal said. "I'm going to scout around."

Mac Traven walked inside and looked around. He felt sick and empty. Ma, pa, . . . Gretchen. Even Jesse. All gone. What kind of a man was this Ashford, if he was the one behind this?

The house looked smaller than he remembered, but there were still curtains in the windows and the rag rugs ma used to make. They had not taken those.

He got out a frying pan and sliced bacon into it. He looked around when Susan came in. "I'm sorry about your dog."

"He was a good dog, Susan. Never bothered anybody. He helped us a lot with the cattle. I never knew him to bite anybody, but I guess when those men grabbed my sister he tried to make a fight."

"What will you do?"

"Go after them, Susan. We will have to go after them."

Dal came in through the open door. "There's a light in the window over at the Wyatts'. When I topped the rise west of here I could just make it out."

"The way their house sets down in the hollow they might have missed it. If Aunt Maddy is over there that might be a good place for Susan to stay."

Susan looked at him, and tears came into her eyes. "You will leave me?"

"Have to, Susan. We've got to chase after those men, and when we catch up there will be shooting. It will be no place for a little girl.

"But you'll love Aunt Maddy. She's not really our aunt, but everybody calls her that. There's only one trouble with it."

Dal looked around from where he was pulling off his boots. "What's that? Aunt Maddy's a great old girl."

Mac looked very serious. "If we leave Susan there we won't know her when we get back. The way Aunt Maddy likes to cook she'll have Susan so fatted up we won't know her. She'd be round as a pumpkin!"

"I would not!"

"Maddy Wyatt sets a good table. She's never so happy as when she's feeding somebody. She likes to bake an' cook, and she's always putting up jars of fruit, vegetables, whatever."

"They're travellin' fast, Mac. Looks to me like they're just hittin' the high spots close to their line of travel. I'd say they're headed for Mexico, and I know that was in Ashford's thinkin'. Go there, build up their strength, and come back."

"He's crazy! The South has had enough of war. So has the North."

"Not according to him, Mac. He's a fanatic. He'll stop at nothing."

"Dal?" When his brother looked up he said, "Dal, what about Kate?"

FOUR

"I've been thinkin' about her. Maybe we should ride into town?"

Mac shook his head. "There's no time, Dal. We'll stop by Maddy's and see if she can take care of Susan. If all's well and she can, then we'll just have to leave word. We're three or four days behind now."

At daybreak they rolled out of their blankets and picked up what they needed. Dal fixed the door and they fastened it shut to keep the weather out.

Maddy Wyatt was in the doorway shading her eyes at them when they came down the slope into the hollow where her ranch-house stood. Aunt Maddy Wyatt was fair, fat, and forty . . . or maybe fifty. She had a wide, friendly smile, rosy cheeks, and a booming laugh.

"Recognized you! I says to myself there's nobody sets a saddle like them Traven boys! Has to be them! And what a relief you're here now. Light an' set!"

"Can't, Maddy. We're ridin' after our folks. What happened here?"

"I don't rightly know what happened at your place. I was out in the brush huntin' a settin' hen that had laid her eggs out yonder when I heard shootin'. I figured it was Injuns, so I fetched my Sharps and bellied down in the ol' rifle-pit up yonder. Sure enough, they come around.

"There was seven of them, mostly in parts of uniforms, but no proper sojers. I know sojers when I see 'em, an' one time or another, I've knowed a-plenty.

"They come down the slope yonder, and I let the ol' Sharps kick dirt in front of them. They pulled up quick, and I got me an idea then they wasn't lookin' for a fight. They wanted all they could git but without a fight.

"They hollered at me but I made 'em no answer. Let 'em worry. I didn't want 'em to know I was a woman alone or that there was only one of me. That ol' rifle-pit was well dug, an' I had me a way out from behind and down into the canyon and the trees behind, an' a good field of fire.

"They hollered an' I said nothin', but when they moved again I put a bullet at one's head. Sorry it was, but I missed. Burned him. Maybe got his ear—I saw some blood on the ground after. Anyway, they taken off.

"I'd had a chance to bunch my stock into the brush, and they could see nothin' worth takin', and they decided it was no use gettin' somebody killed.

"Later, I fetched my horse an' scouted your place. The tracks told me there was a passel of 'em and sure enough, they'd caught your folks by surprise. They shot up your pa real bad and left him for dead. Your ma's taken him to the doctor in Austin. They wounded Jesse, too, but took him along, and they got your sister, Gretchen. They just threw 'em in the back of a wagon with other girls they'd been pickin' up in their raidin'."

Aunt Maddy glanced at Dal. "They had Kate, too. Frank Kenzie tried to put up a fight, but—"

"Kenzie? How's he figure in this?"

"Well," Aunt Maddy glanced at him, "you was reported dead. Ever'body said you'd been killed. Kenzie started comin' around. He's got himself a nice place over east of here, and he was huntin' a wife. He was sparkin' Kate."

Dal swore and spat.

"You can't blame her. You've been gone four years and was supposed to be dead. What's a girl to do?"

"She could wait. She could have give me a chance to get home."

"A dead man? No woman who's as much woman as Kate is going to want a ghost. She wants a man. Not that I'd say Frank Kenzie shaped up alongside of you, but around these parts a girl can't pick an' choose."

"What happened?" Mac demanded.

"Kenzie tried to stop 'em, and one of them slapped him with a six-shooter alongside the head. He taken it an' kept comin', so he was hit a couple of more times. They broke his arm and laid his scalp open and just rode off with Kate."

"Can you take care of Susan for us? She'll tell you what happened. She's the girl of a man I fought alongside."

"Susan? You just bet I will! Mighty lonesome around here sometimes. Susan, you just get down and come in. I got a special room for you, and I've got a barrel of cookies in yonder. Well, most of a barrel, anyway."

Mac caught Susan's hand and squeezed it. "You help Aunt Maddy now. We'll bring your mother back or know the reason why."

Mac led the way south at a spanking trot. It was a country of rolling hills, the grass green with spring-time, and the hills were dotted with clumps of oak.

Later, when watering their horses at a stream, Dal commented, "Wished I had me one o' them Blakeslee Quick-Loaders like you've got. The two of us could fight a war."

"We'll keep our eyes open. Maybe we can find some soldier bound for home who needs a dollar or a drink."

Since the renegades had kept from main trails, hiding in the hills and moving steadily south, they saw travellers only occasionally. Each time they came upon a camp, Mac and Dal studied it with care.

"Six or seven, maybe eight women along," Mac said, "and they keep 'em bunched up and under guard. Whatever he plans to do with them he's not letting them be molested now.

"See here?" Dal indicated several tracks around a separate fire. "Their tracks are plain enough. See the heels? And over here's where a guard was settin'. You can see his heel marks there and where his rifle butt rested on the ground."

"We've gained on 'em," Mac commented. "I figure we're less than three days behind them. Maybe only two."

"Ashford's a soldier, we can't be forgettin' that. He will be havin' a rear-guard out, especially as he will expect to be chased by somebody. We've got to ride mighty careful. Be just like him to set up an ambush."

"That there," Mac commented, "looks like Jesse's

track with the women. See here? He had that busted spur, always hung a little lower than the other. There's the mark of that spur."

"It's been four years," Dal said, "but that surely looks like his track. At least he's up an' around. He'll be watchin' his chance—we know that. I just hope he doesn't take too much risk until we get close up to help."

In the gray of morning they rode west along a deep draw and topped out several miles from the trail. From the ridge Mac used the field glasses he'd brought back from the War.

"Nothin'," he said, "but I say we ride wide of the trail."

They made coffee over a small fire in a hollow under some trees. Neither felt like talking. "I'm dead for sleep," Dal said. "You take first watch?"

Mac Traven was tired. He added a few small sticks to the fire and taking his rifle walked up on the knoll to look around. The night was very still, not a breath of wind. He looked off to the south. Sound could carry a long way on such a night but they were much too far away. Still . . .

The stars were very bright. He listened, ears straining for the slightest sound.

Somewhere off to the south a coyote talked to the night, protesting his loneliness to the stars. Mac got up and walked to a leaning tree, standing beside it.

He reviewed in his mind what they knew of the attack on their family and ranch. There was more to this than had appeared. The man who had wounded Dal had been riding Ranch Baby, and Dal had said the man who shot him had known he was shooting at Traven, so he must have taken part in the raid on the ranch.

Perhaps the man had had a falling-out with Ashford

and had set off on his own when his trail crossed Dal's. There might be others splintering off from Ashford and his crowd, other men eager to kill any Traven who could connect them to the attack on the ranch.

There was trouble in Texas. Further east the Regulators and the Moderators were killing each other, with almost nightly shootings. The Comanches had been raiding, and bandits along the border and from the Neuces country had been raiding ranches, stealing horses and cattle, and generally taking advantage of the fact that most of the young men who might oppose them were still not home from the War.

The Rangers, and there were too few of them, would have their hands full.

Asking help from the sheriff would have been a waste of time, as he did no more than he had to and was no friend to the Travens, anyway. Whatever was done they must do themselves.

On cat feet, he scouted around the camp, pausing to listen several times, and then glancing at the Big Dipper to see what time it was, he went back into the hollow. The pot was on the fire, and he poured a cup. The night was growing cold. He sipped his coffee slowly.

This was the time they should all be working, trying to get the place in shape and brand what cattle were running loose. Times were bad, and they were not going to become financially secure without a lot of hard work. There was no way pa and Jesse could have kept up with the increase in cattle. Branding on the open range was a long, hard job, with much riding. If Kate was still free she and Dal would be setting up for themselves, and Dal would have a share coming.

Mac walked back to the fire and sat down in the shadows facing it. He did not stare into the flames, knowing it would take too long for his eyes to adjust to sudden darkness if someone came up on them. He leaned back against a tree, the Spencer across his lap.

What about pa and ma? He would have felt more comfortable if he and Dal could have taken the time to ride up to Austin to see how pa was recovering. It had to be tough on them, the attack on the ranch, pa getting shot up, not knowing what would become of Jesse and Gretchen, and them thinking Dal was dead too. But he knew that they had made the right decision to keep following Ashford's trail.

The first consideration was to free the captives before they reached Mexico, if possible. Yet what could the two of them do? The camp would be well guarded, and some of the men in that camp were probably as good at scouting as either he or Dal.

"We could use some help," he muttered, half aloud. "We surely could."

But who would help? Maddy had said Kenzie had a broken arm and did not seem too eager, anyway. None of the others had acted like they wished to be involved in any way. Some of them did not like him because he had elected to fight for the Union, and a lot of the people around town now were strangers. Newcomers had been drifting in since the War, without ties to the community. In the old days one man's trouble was trouble for all, and all pitched in and helped no matter whether it was an Indian fight, a barn raising, or a buffalo hunt.

He added fuel to the fire, moved back into the trees, and listened to the night . . . all was still. It was time he called Dal to take over, but his mind was in no condition for sleep. There were too many problems.

When they came up with the renegades they must first scout the camp. His field glasses would help in that, but he must use them with care and never when a reflection might be seen. If they could study the lay-out, there was a chance they might Injun into camp, free the girls, and get away.

Seven or eight girls? No chance. One of them would bump against something, fall, gasp or something. It would be the same with seven or eight men. The odds were against easing that many out of camp. One, even two, but not seven.

From the tracks he had observed, the girls all seemed to be riding in the wagon.

Cut the wagon out and get away with it? Maybe when the marchers were all scattered out? There would be times, there always were on such treks, when going over a hill, through a draw, or something when most of the men would be out of sight of the wagon. That was something to be hoped for, but one could not plan that way.

Some of the men with Ashford were guerillas of the type who rode with Quantrill or Bloody Bill Anderson—bad men, but good as any Injun when it came to working rough country in a fight.

He walked over and checked the horses. All was quiet. The horses were in good shape, and he and Dal would push hard today, closing the gap.

He went to another tree, further from the fire, and sat down. A voice spoke from the blankets. "What's the matter? You want to be on watch all night?"

"Figured you were tired."

"I'm tired, but so are you. Come on now, you get some sleep. You ought to know I always wake up on time."

Mac walked to his blankets and sat down, pulling off his boots, then his gun belt and spare pistol. His hat beside him, his head on his saddle, he looked up at the stars through the leaves. There was too much to think about, and he was never going to get to sleep. Dal might just as well have . . .

He opened his eyes to the smell of coffee and the sound of a crackling fire. He sat up abruptly. Dal was at the fire and glanced over at him, his eyes twinkling. "I'd say for a man who wasn't tired you did a mighty good job of sleeping."

Mac shook out his boots to dislodge any stray scorpions, lizards, or tarantulas that might have taken refuge during the night.

He slung on his gun belt and walked down to the trickle of water beside which they had camped and splashed water on his face. He squatted beside the branch and after a minute, splashed more cold water on his eyes and rinsed his hands, then flipped the water from his face with his fingers and wiped his fingers dry on his pants.

"Coffee and bread," Dal said. "We've got to come up with some rations, partner."

"You're telling me? My stomach thinks my throat's been cut." He bit off a piece of the bread and took a swallow of the black coffee. "We're going to close in on them tonight. I've had enough of this. We've got to get that wagon away from them when all the girls are in it."

"Take some doin'. And hard to get away, after."

"You thought about something? Happy Jack Traven had a place down thisaway."

"When he was out of jail."

"I think maybe we could use him. He had friends among all them Neuces outlaws, too. Remember? He was always takin' up for them, feedin' 'em, hidin' 'em from time to time? We could use some help."

A pebble rattled among the rocks, and Dal rolled over behind a fallen tree. Mac's Spencer slid forward.

"Nice of you boys to remember me, an' that coffee sure smells good!"

Happy Jack Traven wore a battered black hat and a smile on a face seamed by sun, wind, and years. "Mac? Put down that gun. You wouldn't be shootin' an old man, would you?"

"Come in an' set. You'll never get old, Jack. You're too mean. Where'd you steal that horse?"

"Now, Mac, that's unkind. You know I never stole no horse unless I needed him. This here's one your pappy give me."

FIVE

"How did you find us?"

"Been watchin' for you. Your ma sent word about what happened at your place. You didn't think I was goin' to tackle that outfit all by myself, did you? I said to myself, says I, 'Them boys will come a high-tailin' it after their sister, an' they'll surely need help.' So I been settin' an' waitin' while sort of keepin' track of that outfit."

"How far ahead are they?"

"Last night, about two days. Looks to me like they've taken a notion to go over to the Gulf Coast. At least, they've changed direction. Turned almost at right angles just after some gent rode into their camp on a paint pony. He was not a stranger to them, either. He just rode right in and went straight to the boss-man."

"I figured they were at least three days ahead."

"They been settin'. I figure they were waitin' for whatever this gent on the paint had to tell them.

"You know, most of those folks down below that border are mighty fine people, but just like with us, there's some that hangin' is too good for. There's folks down there will pay good prices for women, preferably white women, blondes at the top of the list.

"They'll buy men, too, black or white, to work in the mines. They don't let the officials know what's goin' on, or they find one they can pay off. Most of them live far out in the hills, and some are bandits, operatin' both sides of the border. I figure that's where they're headed for."

"Why would they head for the Gulf Coast?"

"Only thing that makes sense is that they figure to meet a ship over there. You know there's some fellers around who were smuggling slaves in through the bayous to New Orleans and the like. With the end of the War they're out of business, unless they find something else. They'll stop at nothing.

"Importing slaves into the country has been illegal for years, but they smuggled 'em in. The way I hear it this Ashford feller used to deal in smuggled slaves now and again. Take 'em to his plantation, let 'em work for a few weeks, then sell them off like they'd been here for years.

"If that's true he would know who to get in touch with if he had something to sell. Trust a slave dealer to know where slaves, even white slaves, could be sold."

"How could a man justify that sort of thing? What kind of man could he be?" Mac said.

Happy Jack glanced at him over his cup. "There's some folks will justify anything if it will make them a dollar. Commonest excuse is that if they don't do it somebody else will. It's high time folks started ostracizing anybody who makes a dishonest dollar. Worst thing about crime is the kind of people you have to associate with."

Mac Traven checked the Spencer. Happy Jack watched him, saying, "There's a town east of here. South an' east, rightly speaking. If a feller had some money he could pick up some grub, an' maybe a little news."

"What town?"

"Well, we gotta choice, sort of. There's Victoria—that's closest—then there's others further along. I'd say we ride into Victoria and have a look around, buy ourselves some grub an' maybe see how the wind is blowin'.

"Since the War ended there ain't been much of what you could call law in Texas. I hear tell there's a Union general bringin' some troops into Galveston, but he ain't here yet so far's I know."

"Sounds all right to me," Dal said, "but I surely hate to leave this trail, even for a few hours."

"My feelin' is they'll be headin' the same way, only I think they'll fight shy of Victoria. Here in the last twenty-five years or so, ever since about 1840 the way I hear it, Victoria's become more German than Spanish. Lot of settlers moved in. Now a lot of those folks have Union sentiments, at least so I've heard. I think Ashford may ride into Victoria, but not with his women and his wagons."

Mac Traven had ideas about that, but he kept still, thinking it out. Southwest of Victoria, if he recalled correctly, was the Guadalupe River, with a thick stand of pecan, cypress, and oak along its course. There was a good place to hole up and rest, with grass for the stock and plenty of water. If Ashford or some of his crowd were riding into town they would certainly leave the camp on the Guadalupe. He said as much to Dal. "My bet is we will lose no time at all, and may gain a little,

but step easy and talk polite. These folks don't trifle
with the law. They take it serious."

Cattle grazed on the salt meadows as they neared
the town. Here and there a farm wagon headed toward
town. The road was gray with the crushed shells of an
old sea, whether natural or dumped to fill mud holes,
Mac could not guess. The town looked gray and weather-
beaten. There were scattered trees, and back from the
main street there were several unusually attractive
houses.

At the livery barn Mac lighted a cigar, and glancing
at the hostler, a gray-haired, weathered old Texan, he
asked, "Any other strangers riding in today?"

"Not that come here." The Texan accepted a light for
the cigar Mac offered. "Seen a few Confederate uniforms around."

"My brother fought for the Confederacy," Mac said
casually. "I went along with old Sam Houston's thinking."

"Me, too, although I'm a Texian from way back. Lost
an uncle at Goliad, and I was with them who chased the
Comanches after they destroyed Victoria an' Linnville.
They run off about two thousand horses, killed a lot of
folks, and headed back for the Plains."

They talked quietly for a while of Texas, the hard
times, and what might be expected from a carpet-bag
governor.

"Bad outfit camped down on the Guadalupe," Mac
commented. "Some renegades who claim to be Confederates. Some of them were, most weren't."

"Know them kind. These fellers I seen this morning,
they're yonder in the saloon right this minute. A couple
of them are over to the store." He took the cigar from
his teeth and pointed with a middle finger. "Those are
their horses yonder."

Dal looked over at him. "Maybe we should go read 'em from the Book."

"Not yet," Mac objected. "Buy what we need first, pack it on the horses." He turned to his uncle. "Happy, do any of those boys know you?"

"I don't reckon."

"Why don't you go in there and keep an eye on them. Have a drink, listen to what you can hear.

"Dal? Why don't you sort of hang around outside in case of trouble. I've got the money, so I'll do a fast job of buyin' what we need."

Mac watched the two cross the street separately; then he went to the store.

It was a large room with tables stacked with cooking-ware, shirts, pants, vests. At the counter were two men, both wearing Confederate coats. Both were unshaven and dusty from travel. Both men wore guns in holsters.

"Sorry." The clerk was a man in a white shirt, smooth-shaven except for mustache and side-burns. "Confederate money is no longer good. I cannot accept it."

"What d' you mean, no good? I fit for the Cause. They paid me this here money."

"I am truly sorry, gentlemen, but you will have to have gold. That's the way we have to pay for what we buy."

"Now looky here," the speaker was a stocky man with a beard streaked with gray, "we ain't huntin' trouble but we got thirty men down on the river who say this here money is good. You want them to come into town to show you?"

The clerk smiled. "You have thirty men? We have three hundred men here who can bear arms, and who do. These men grew up fighting Comanches. You may bring your thirty men in whenever you wish, and some of you may even ride out, if you are quick enough."

The clerk was still smiling but his eyes were cold. "I would suggest, gentlemen, that you bring gold to do your buying or forget it."

Mac stood by, quietly watching. One of the men glanced at him, at his Cavalry hat, started to turn away, then looked back. "Don't I know you?"

"I don't believe so," Mac spoke gently. "I am careful about my company."

"*What?* What did you say?"

The clerk had started away; now he paused. "Please," he said to Mac. "I understand how you feel, but not in here, please."

"What did you say?" The man with the beard was belligerent. "Just repeat that!"

"Are you with that bunch camped over on the Guadalupe? In all my born days I never did see so many different brands on a herd of cattle. Why, I recall one of those brands from away up on the Red River!"

"We been buyin' cattle," the bearded man replied sullenly.

"With Confederate money?" Mac asked gently. "Your business must be very good, or you are very persuasive."

"Frank," one of the other men said, "we got to get back to camp." He caught the bearded man by the arm. "Let's go."

Frank pulled his arm away. "Just a minute. I want to know what this man's gettin' at."

Mac Traven smiled pleasantly, his eyes twinkling. "I am simply interested, that's all. When I see a wild-looking bunch of men driving cattle with mixed brands, and guarding a wagon loaded with young girls, I just wonder what's going on."

"You seen no such thing!" the second man said angrily. "We're just a travellin' with our folks, that's all! Come on, Frank. They don't like the color of our money. Let's go elsewhere."

The clerk turned to Mac. "Is what you said true?"

"They're a bad bunch," Mac said. "They're driving cattle picked up all along the way. Most of them are former guerillas, and they have captured some young women.

"I didn't mean to start trouble in your store but neither did I want them to get supplies here."

Mac smiled again. "I have gold, and I would like to buy."

When his order was filled he picked up the sacks and slung them over his left shoulder, moving to the door, where he paused.

Dal was still loitering in front of the saloon, but now he had moved from the place where he had been standing and was on the edge of the walk, looking toward him.

Glancing left and right, Mac saw three men gathered, two of them the men he had talked to in the store. The one named Frank was resisting arguments by the other two.

Mac hesitated, then stepped out on the walk. He would have to pass by the three men to reach the livery stable where their horses were. He glanced at Dal, and Dal nodded. Mac stepped off the board-walk and started toward them.

If shooting started there were other men inside the saloon. This was not going to be easy. There was no way it could be easy.

He was within six feet of them before they saw him. Frank jerked away from the others. "There's that Blue Belly, son-of-a—!"

A dozen men along the street turned at the loud

voice. Frank lunged for him, and Mac dropped his two heavy sacks in front of him, drawing his Remington at the same time.

Frank stumbled and fell over the dropped sacks, and the other two were looking at Mac's gun. He stepped back one step to keep Frank covered also.

"I suggest," Mac spoke quietly, "that if you gentlemen wish to live a few days longer, you leave, now."

Frank was getting up, very slowly. He looked at Mac Traven and then at the gun. He kept his hands wide from his body.

"When you get back to your camp," Mac continued, "you tell Ashford to free those girls he has taken, to free every one of them, unharmed. Tell him that word comes from Major Mac Traven."

"I don't see no army," Frank sneered.

Mac Traven smiled. "I don't need an army, Frank, but what I need, I've got."

Suddenly three men burst from the saloon, then pulled up sharply, looking at the scene in the street before them. Happy Jack Traven emerged from the saloon behind them, a cup of coffee in his left hand.

"If I were you," Mac said, "I'd deliver that message and then get yourself out of the way. This is a big, wide open country. You don't have to go to Mexico."

A slender man in a black coat, who was one of the three from the saloon, stepped down off the porch. "What's going on here?" he asked pleasantly.

"Nothing very exciting," Mac replied. "These gentlemen have been stirring up a little trouble, and I've just suggested they leave town before somebody gets hurt.

"I also suggested they free those young women they've captured, and free them unharmed."

"I am sure there's been a mistake," the man said

smoothly. "I have been travelling with these men, who are cattle drovers."

"Whose cattle are they driving?" Mac said. "I saw a collection of brands from ranches north and somewhat west of here, but no road brand. I suggest we ask the local sheriff to inspect that herd and your papers, sir."

The man in the black coat glanced around. There were twenty-five or thirty people standing around listening. Under his breath he swore bitterly. This was all they needed, to stir up trouble with these people now.

"Of course," he said politely, "I'd be glad to agree. We are under a good deal of pressure for time, unhappily. We have some sickness in the wagons and wish to get our young people to the care of a physician."

"I am sure there is a good doctor in Victoria, and I would be glad to pay for his attentions to those of you who are sick." Mac was very cool. He dropped the Remington into its holster. "Why go away from this nice town when you have illness?"

"Let's get out of here!" Frank said irritably. "This isn't gettin' us nowhere!"

The other two men stepped down off the board-walk and came toward the man in black, but only he observed Happy Jack Traven and Dal stepping off the porch behind them.

"We must go, but come whenever you are ready, and by all means, bring your doctor."

He bowed, turned, and walked toward his horse, the others following.

Mac Traven hesitated. Could he get a doctor and the law to go with him? And could they do it in time? He had no doubt the caravan would be moving within minutes of the arrival of these men in the camp on the Guadalupe.

A tall gray-haired man came from the board-walk. "What was that all about?" he asked.

Briefly, Mac Traven explained, then added, "They are heavily armed, good fighting men, and there are at least thirty of them. Nor will they stand for a search or for any doctor. In all fairness, I have to warn you of that. A search will show kidnapped women, stolen horses and cattle, and a thoroughly vicious bunch of men."

"What are you going to do?"

"Follow them, get those women away from them, and hopefully the cattle as well. These are dangerous men and must be stopped."

"They have done no harm here, and our sheriff is in San Antonio. You might try for volunteers, but I doubt if you'd get many. It is not their fight, and this is a busy time for all here."

As the man walked away Happy Jack swore. "You should have killed that Frank," he said irritably. "We had 'em boxed."

"And endanger innocent people? When lead starts flying it is usually bystanders who get hurt. No, I can wait. When a man uses a gun he should be aware of the consequences."

"What do we do now?"

"We follow them, we get the girls back. We stampede their cattle, we delay them, we watch our chance to get that wagon-load of women. Let's go!"

SIX

Kate Connery was working close to their wagon when she saw the riders return from Victoria. They went at once to the canvas awning under which Colonel Ashford waited.

She heard a mutter of voices and then one slightly louder, "Said he was Major Mac Traven. Sounded like he figured you'd know the name. There was at least one other man with him, maybe two. The one I was sure of was tall an' dark, like Traven himself. Could be a brother."

There was a mutter of voices then, and ". . . tellin' ever'body. That storekeeper, he said they could mount three hundred riflemen, words to that effect. I figure he lied."

"I believe he did not," Ashford said sharply. "If you know the history of Victoria you would know it has been attacked by Indians on several occasions, and they

49

are prepared to resist. I think, gentlemen, we had better pull out. This is no time to have trouble."

Kate went around behind the wagon, out of sight. Her heart was pounding. *Mac Traven here!* And that other one sounded like Dal, but Dal was dead . . . or was he?

She went to the back of the wagon and looked at her sister Dulcie and Gretchen Traven lying with the others. "Dulcie?" she whispered.

One of the girls sat up, and Kate whispered, "We'll be leaving soon. Don't make any trouble, and be very quiet. We've got to watch our chances."

"What chances?" Dulcie said. "They haven't given us any kind of a chance!"

"Dulcie? Mac is out there. He's got a man with him, maybe more. We've got to be very quiet, very obedient, and watch our chances. Mac will do something. I know he will." She paused. "I think Dal is with him."

"You know that isn't true!" Gretchen said. "Dal was killed!"

"We *heard* that, but we don't *know*. I overheard them talking, and they said one of the other men was tall and dark and looked like Mac."

"What shall we do?"

"Be alert. That's all we can do. Mac will do something. I know he will!"

A stocky man with black hair and an unshaven face came by. "Get into the wagon," he said roughly. "We're pullin' out."

"Where are we going now?" Kate asked.

He paused. He had been one of the kindest of them, although his tone was always rough. "You'll get some sea air, maybe. You ever seen the sea?"

"No, I haven't."

"Neither have I, but they tell me we're gittin' close.

Git in that wagon now and don't you make no trouble. There's a passel of very touchy men out yonder."

There was a rattle of trace chains and the sound of horses moving. Listening, they heard all the sounds of a hurried breaking of camp, then a low-voiced "Ho!"

The wagon began to move, rocking and rolling over numerous obstructions. "Over the bank!" she heard someone direct, and the wagon tilted sharply back. A whip cracked, and the wagon lurched forward and up as they clung to the sides to keep from falling in a heap at the back of the wagon. Then it lurched over the crest, and they were rolling along.

"We're going to the Gulf," she whispered to Cordelia Atherton, the woman next to her. "I don't know why."

Mrs. Atherton was silent for a moment, and then she said, "That means a boat or something. There's no good trail along the Gulf that doesn't run into town. Corpus is down there."

"A boat?"

Mrs. Atherton's voice was dry. "Kate, you'd better understand this. If your friend Mac doesn't come up with something we're headed for slavery."

"Slavery?" Kate's voice shrilled a little. "What do you mean? That's over, and besides, we're white."

"There were white slaves long before any blacks were enslaved, except by their own people. We had a preacher told us about it. Even the word slave came from 'Slav' because some of the early Roman slaves were from Slavic countries. There's places where white women bring a good price. And why else would they go to the Gulf?"

There were few sounds except for the rolling rumble of the wagons, the occasional crack of a whip, and periodically a muffled curse.

Once when the wagon stopped to give the horses a

chance to catch their breath, a horseman rode up along-side the driver.

"River up ahead. No idea how deep, but might be swimmin' water this time of year."

"Where we headed for?"

The answer was lower. "Little place. Copano."

"Never heard of it."

"Damn few have! That's why we're goin' there. Ain't but a handful of folks there, and nobody's liable to make trouble. Anyway, we'll not be in town, jus' close by."

He rode off, and after a minute the wagon started on. Mrs. Atherton spoke again. "I'm worried about my little girl. Had to leave her."

"*Leave* her?"

"You think I'd bring her into this? Her pappy should be home from the war by now. If not, there's neighbors if she'll get out an' walk. I'd no notion of bringin' her into this. Although I wasn't looking for slavery. I'd expected rape and maybe killing, but not this."

"Mac's out there. He'll do something."

"What can one man do?"

"Mac can do a lot. He was a Texas Ranger four years. Rode with Rip Ford, Captain Jack Hays, and them. He's the best man with a gun I ever did see, unless it was Dal."

A man's voice broke in. "Dal?"

Kate shot a glance over to where Jesse Traven lay in the wagon.

"Ssh!"

The driver turned his head. "He comin' to? Was that him I heard?"

"He's delirious," Kate said, "talkin' in his sleep. He thinks he's back up in north Texas."

Leaning over close to Jesse's ear she whispered, "Mac's out there somewhere. Dal maybe with him. They said there were at least two, and the description sounded like Dal." Jesse had been wounded in the raid but tied up and brought along with the women. He was only just now showing signs of returning to full consciousness.

For a long time they rocked and rolled across the country, though often it was flat for some distance. Then they went over low hills, if such they could be called.

Kate sat quiet, listening. *If only she had a knife!* Something to cut Jesse loose! She had to keep her eyes open. She might find something, some broken glass, anything!

She smelled water and foliage. The rider stopped by. "Ain't so deep. I'll ride in ahead of you. She ain't more than belly deep for the horses."

"When we goin' to sleep?" the driver demanded. "I'm t'rd."

"Who ain't? Ashford, he's meetin' somebody down by the water, some gun-runner or whatever. We got to get there, make our deal, get shut of these women, and head back inland and for Mexico."

She glanced at the driver. She could see the butt of his pistol, but it did no good for he had a thong over the hammer, and from watching him she knew it was a tight fit. Anyway, if they did escape, where could they go? This was open country, salt grass meadow as well as she could tell in the dark, and no place to hide.

She dozed off and slept. It was almost dawn when the stopping of the wagon awakened her. The wind had picked up a little, and she could hear it blowing through leaves that rustled.

"Get some rest," somebody was saying. "Ain't got more'n ten mile to go."

She could hear them taking the teams away. She crawled to the back of the wagon, trying to avoid the sleepers, and peered out. It was almost daybreak. She could see some trees and a lot of willows, and hear the soft rustle and gurgle of water.

If she could just get out now, slip away and run for it! Why, it might be full daylight before they knew she was gone. But where could she go? Where was she? And how could she leave the girls? They needed her, although this other woman, the mother who left her daughter behind, seemed steady and not at all afraid.

The woman spoke now, very low. "I'm not gettin' on a ship, no matter what."

"Trust Mac. He'll come."

Kate had to trust him. There was nobody else. To escape now, if it were only herself to think of, would be her best chance. The closer they got to the water the harder it would be.

Jesse was feeling better. They had been making believe he was still unconscious, but even so the men had tied his hands and feet.

Now, at this camp, she had to find something, anything. They were closer to the sea, and she might find a piece of a seashell.

Ashford's voice interrupted her thoughts. "You can all get out of the wagon now, but stay close. I won't be responsible for my men if one of you wanders off alone."

Slowly, Kate got down from the wagon, then helped Gretchen.

"Your brother still alive?" Ashford asked.

"He's not my brother. He's Gretchen's brother."

"You seem to know them well."

"They were neighbors. I knew the family well."

"Traven? Is that the name? Did you know a Major Mac Traven?"

"He was no major when I knew him. He was Sergeant Mac Traven of the Texas Rangers."

"You don't say? I have heard the Rangers were a hard lot."

"They had to be. It was wild country, and they fought Comanches, Kiowas, and outlaws 'most every day."

Ashford was thoughtful. Mac Traven had been a Texas Ranger, and he knew their reputation from the Mexican War and since. One could not take such men lightly. Still, he was alone or with just one man, and what could two men do against his lot? These were not the men he would have chosen; most of them were renegades and guerillas, but they were first-class fighting men and could handle themselves in wild country.

He tried putting himself in Traven's place. What would he do? What could he do?

He would try to get help. There might be former Rangers in the area. Ashford walked away from the wagon and looked into the slowly flowing stream. A small log lay across it almost at water level, and some brush and debris had piled up there, some twigs, branches, an old bottle, and what looked like a fence-post. Yet he was not thinking of that. He was trying to plan what he must do.

Remain here now, leaving only just before dark? Or chance going on to the coast at daylight?

Copano Bay was a completely land-locked harbor, except for the opening into Aransas Bay, which was protected from the waves of the Gulf by St. Joseph's Island. Copano had never amounted to much as a harbor, but some vessels did come there.

One more day and he'd be rid of the women and girls. He thought of that, then hastily turned his thoughts away. After all, he needed arms and he needed money, and people always suffered one way or the other. He had dealt in slaves before this, although the others had always been black. And he had only bought or sold them for his own plantation.

Plantation! He swore under his breath. All gone now, destroyed in the War. His stock had been run off and the house and stables burned. Even the slaves' quarters were gone.

Just wait! He'd have arms again. He could help Maximilian and come out of that with a good bit of money and arms. Perhaps he might even get some actual help from the Prince. Hadn't they owned Louisiana at one time? And didn't La Salle make a sort of claim on Texas?

He might persuade him to help or at least recruit some of the mercenaries who were supporting him. He would need men . . . of course, southerners would rally to the Cause. None of them had wished to surrender. Oh, here and there was some malcontent or coward, but most of them had wished to fight on had it not been for Lee.

Surrendering! Handing his sword to that upstart Custer, of all people!

Yet in Mexico, where he would be safe, he could recruit an army and start north, retaking the country as he went. He might even sail to Mobile Bay and strike north from there, following the Tennessee River right into the heart of the South! He would ride back into Richmond a conquering hero.

He walked back to the camp, glancing toward Kate's wagon. Now there was a woman. If he talked to her . . . she was bright and very practical. She would see the light soon enough, and after all, what choice could she have?

His tent had been raised, and he walked back into it, pulled off his gloves, and threw his hat on the table. He got out his map case and opened it, spreading the maps on the table.

Copano Bay, Lamar Peninsula . . . the mouth of Copano Creek. He was not exactly sure where the town was. He knew of the place only by reputation.

Now, he leaned over the map—right at the mouth of Copano Creek, if . . .

Kate built their own small fire and fixed what food was provided. It was not much.

When they had eaten she went down to the bank of the little stream to wash the dishes. She cleaned them, then straightened up to take the kink out of her back. Looking down stream, she saw the pole that lay across the river and the debris.

She also saw the bottle. . . .

SEVEN

Morning came with low clouds and only a hint of red in the sky. From the shelter of trees the three riders looked across at Ashford's camp. A sleepy-looking man was rounding up the small herd of cattle, some fifty head.

Through his glasses Mac could see only one or two men moving about. One was harnessing a team. Another was at the fire.

"Walk your horses until we're close," Happy Jack suggested. "See that gully there? We can come up out of there, but don't get carried away with shootin' to scare the cattle an' forget to hold some lead for those fellers."

"You ready?" Dal asked.

They walked their horses through the brush to the draw, then turned along the draw, which would bring them parallel to the camp and the herd. "That white

58

rock?" Mac asked. "There by that lightning-struck cypress? What say we come out right there? Stampede their cows and ride like Hell for that clump yonder?"

Mac drew his holstered gun. "Careful you don't get stampeded yourself," Jack whispered. "There's a big bird down here. They call it a whooping crane. If you ain't ready for it you can get scared out of your britches!"

Mac touched his lips with his tongue. The fog was lifting. The morning would be bright and sunny. It worried him that the camp was now out of sight and a dozen men might be waiting with rifles. The chances were against it, but a man never knew.

Happy Jack pulled up near the white rock. "I'll go up until I can see over the edge. When I give the word, come a shootin', but not until we see the cattle."

He climbed his horse up the sloping bank and drew up, holding an open palm behind him to keep them back. Then he spoke. "Herd's not more'n fifty yards off. When you top the ridge, give 'em Hell!"

Their horses scrambled through the sand. Suddenly the last of the fog lifted, and the camp lay bright and clear before them. A man had just walked out of a tent and was stretching. The team had reached the wagon, and another man was bent over reaching for the trace chain.

Happy Jack let go with a wild cowboy yell and jumped his horse toward them, firing a shot, but he did not fire into the air, pulling down instead on the man with the cattle.

Charging and yelling, the three raced at the startled cattle, which took one look and broke into a wild run, right through camp.

The stretching man leaped aside as a wild longhorn

lunged at him. The man tripped over a camp-chair and fell sprawling. Another man scrambled for a rifle. The man at the trace chain turned, surprised, and in that moment his team, harness and all, was gone!

The sleeping camp exploded into action. Men scrambled for their rifles. Others ran to escape the charging cattle. The teamster rushed after his running team, swearing.

The cattle, thoroughly frightened, stampeded through the camp and headed out across the salt meadow, eyes distended, horns bobbing!

Dal was the first at the grove, turning quickly to fire, keeping his shots away from the wagon.

A moment and it was over. Dust hung in the air; and men were rushing out with rifles while others were putting out the scattered fire. From the grove, they looked back.

"Anybody hurt?" Mac asked.

"That feller with the cows is hurt," Happy Jack said grimly. "Figured there was no use wastin' a bullet, so I fired right into him. Got him in the belly, an' if you ask me he won't be settin' up for breakfast! Not this morning!"

They were a good hundred yards from the camp. "Let's go," Mac suggested. "They'll be firing into this clump of trees, and we're liable to get singed."

Keeping the trees between them and the camp, they rode away, dropping down behind a row of sand dunes, low dunes but offering cover. A dozen of the cattle walked ahead of them, and Happy Jack chuckled. "Take 'em awhile to round up their beef, if they ever do. We shook 'em up some."

"Won't be so lucky again," Dal said. "Now they'll keep a closer watch."

The country before them offered little cover, but there were low places and occasional clumps of trees. Mac glanced back but could see nothing but a few scattered cattle and horses.

They rode on, watching the country with care. It was not until they reached some willows along a creek that they pulled up. "Might's well have some grub ourselves," Happy Jack suggested. "It'll take them most of an hour to get goin'."

They gathered a few twigs and boiled coffee while chewing on beef jerky. "That's a bad outfit," Mac commented, "and we'd best not take them lightly. They'll be hunting us."

"They ain't got too much time," Jack said. "They've got that ship to meet. Least that's what seems likely."

Their fire left no smoke in the sky, and their cover, while light, was sufficient. They squatted on their heels drinking coffee and watching the country around. Dal's muscles were stiff, and he moved with care because of his wound. Although he was almost well now, he had to be aware of his weakness.

The light fog that had drifted over the salt meadows and marshes before dawn had largely disappeared. The sun was bright, but the three men at the fire were tired. "Dal? You'd better catch yourself some shut-eye while there's a chance."

"Maybe you're right." Dal eased himself back on the grass and was almost instantly asleep.

"He caught a bad one," Mac said. "Lost a lot of blood."

"This here's a bad time to be in a fight," Jack grumbled. "Times are bad, there's no market for beef, and with the armies comin' home there'll be three men for every job. If I had two-bits to buy seed I'd go to farmin'."

"Two-bits wouldn't get you very far."

"It would buy a packet o' seeds. It's a start. Mac, I'm worried about those girls. That's a mean outfit. Right now Ashford seems to be in control, but suppose he gets shot or whatever? Those girls wouldn't have a chance."

He removed his hat and wiped the sweat-band. "Mac, you better catch yourself twenty minutes or so. I'll stand watch."

"Well—" Mac stretched out, hat over his eyes, and Happy Jack refilled his cup and scanned the country around. From where they sat their fire was screened by the low place where they had camped and some tall reeds growing in the water, as well as by willows along the creek. Open country was all around them.

Three men against thirty? And two of them had too much conscience.

"Well," Jack muttered, "that never bothered me much, not when there's fightin' to do." A good prairie fire, now, would set them by the ears, but impossible because of the girls. Whatever he thought of must take them into consideration.

"That Kate now," he muttered, "she'd always had a good head on her shoulders. If I could just get inside her head! She's thinkin' right now. She's figurin', but on what? What can she do?"

Not quite five miles away Kate Connery was watching the teamster bringing back the four-horse team from the brush, and she was thinking the same thing. There was little time. The Gulf Coast was right over there. She could smell the sea, and it needed no special awareness to understand that once aboard a ship they would have small chance to escape. What was to be done, if anything, must be done now.

"Dulcie," she said, "pass the word along, and *whisper* when you do it. Tell them to be ready for anything. I don't know what we will do, but it will have to happen soon."

"The boys are out there," Gretchen said hopefully.

"There are only three of them. At least that's all we saw. What can they do?"

Sitting in the wagon they listened to the angry talk outside. "Was I Ashford," somebody was saying, "I'd waste no time with the women. Nor tryin' to trade for guns. I'd start movin' toward Laredo, and I'd hit ever' ranch in between. I'd steal every head of stock they've got, take their guns and whatever money they have, and drive right on into Mexico.

"Ol' Maximilian would make us a deal for those cows, believe me. An' meanwhile we'd have the women for ourselves."

"Leave it to him. He's smart. He knows what he's doin'."

"Maybe. An' maybe he wants the women for hisself. Maybe he'll sell us out an' take off aboard that ship, or whatever. I don't trust him. I don't trust nobody."

"Maybe you're right, Frank. Maybe not. I don't know about ships, and I can't figure just what Ashford has in mind, but he's got us this far."

"Toward what?" Frank asked. There was no reply.

Kate peered out through a slit in the canvas. Some of the cattle had been gathered and some of the horses brought back, and Ashford came riding up. "All right," he spoke quietly, "we're moving out. I've put scouts out ahead of us, and flankers. We'll get those Traven boys next time they show."

The driver cracked his whip, and the teams leaned into their harness. The wagons moved. Riders, rifles in hand, moved out to the flanks.

What could Dal and Mac do against so many?

Their progress was slow. There were two wagons, one loaded with food supplies and loot, the other carrying the women. But the salt meadows, easy enough for horses, often had areas of deep sand. Coupled with the late start, they had made but four miles by noon.

Ashford rode up alongside the wagon, and Kate thought he was about to speak to her when a rider appeared. "Seen some tracks, Colonel. Three riders, headin' off to the southwest."

"West?" he was puzzled. "Why west?"

Were they going for help? He knew nothing about Major Mac Traven, but Dal Traven he knew well, and Dal was a first-class fighting man, a daring rider and an expert with any kind of weapon.

The town of Refugio lay off to the west, and they might have friends there.

For a few minutes Ashford considered that, but finally came to the conclusion that by the time they returned with help—if they had, indeed, gone for help— he would be on the ship and away.

He had been a fool to hurry so. With the times what they were he could have recruited an army. So many men were returning home to ruined plantations, empty houses, and no possible way out of the economic trap created by the War's end.

There were many men in the South who felt as he did, and just as many who were prepared for anything that promised three meals a day and a horse to ride. Ashford was well aware that some of the wilder groups of his men were for raiding all the way to the border and escaping across it with thousands of horses and all else they could steal.

At the moment there was no force in Texas that could resist them. The Rangers had largely been disbanded during the War, and what remained would be insufficient to stop a movement of the kind considered. Moreover, there were a good many Texans who would join with them.

The cotton market was gone for the time being, although once things settled down the British ships would be returning to pick up cotton for the mills of Manchester and other centers. In the meantime there was nothing. There were millions of cattle, of course, and there would soon be a huge market in the East, where most of the beef, even the milk cows, had been killed for food during the War. But how to get that cattle there? The Mississippi lay across their route, a seemingly impassable barrier.

The wagons rolled on, the riders held out on the far flanks. Occasionally when he topped out on one of the low sand-hills he could glimpse the sea, the blue waters of the Gulf. It was not far.

Ashford glanced back. Nothing followed them. He had done well to get these men across that much country without being attacked, and it was almost over.

The girls . . . for a moment he felt a twinge of guilt . . . would bring a nice price below the border. The guilt returned, and he felt himself flushing. What would some of his friends say? Did the end justify the means? He would have guns, he would return with a conquering army and free the South once more. He would drive the hated Blue Bellies back north of the Ohio and keep them there.

He would be a hero, the savior. He might even be elected president of the new Confederacy. If a dozen or so women contributed to the cause it was well worth it, and where else could he get money? Money was what he needed.

Some of his men spoke of raiding ranchos, but Ashford was no fool. Cash money had always been in short supply on the Texas frontier, and what had been saved would have been used up in the four years of the War. There would be little or no money.

The British had always been friendly to the South. Once he had an army he could get them to send ships to transport them north. Maybe it would be better to land closer, to come ashore at Charleston or even at Newport News.

He would not need over a thousand men to start, for others would flock to his banner. He would strike so swiftly there would be no chance to gather forces against him. It would be a complete surprise, and by that time the Union Army would have been disbanded.

It was a glorious dream, but one Ashford believed in and was sure he could accomplish.

Only hours remained. They would rendezvous with the ship, obtain arms, rid themselves of the women, and start to gather their strength.

Or maybe they, too, should go aboard the ship, go south to Tampico, and having landed there, build their strength and return from there?

He must try to make a deal with whoever had brought the arms and money. He could go aboard, make a place for his men . . . yes, that could be it.

They could sleep on deck, cook their own food if need be. And he would be gone.

If any pursuit came from Refugio or anywhere

he would seem to have vanished into the coastal mists.

He would erase the tracks, leave nothing for the Travens to find.

Good! That was the way he would do it.

EIGHT

Standing among the willows along the creek Mac Traven watched the wagons move out. The country was too open. There would be no chance to cut off one wagon and get away with it, and their time was running out. Once the women got aboard ship the Travens would have no chance.

Rounding up help was out of the question. In the first place, they knew nobody in this part of Texas, and spring was a worrisome time, when people had to get their crops in. Nor was there time. The Gulf could be little more than ten miles away.

Ten miles! Even in the sand and the swampy land, which seemed to alternate around here, they should make it by sundown, and if the ship was there they would be gone. It was now or never.

Dal and Jack moved up beside him. "Ain't much time," Jack said. "We got to do something."

"We get ourselves killed," Dal said, "and they got no chance at all. That's a mean bunch. They aren't going to run, and nobody's going to scare them. They've been through the mill, and they can shoot. We've been mighty lucky so far."

"We've got to do something!" Jack growled irritably.

"They're holding further west than I expected. Doesn't seem like they're headed for San Antonio Bay."

"Copano," Jack said. "It's a mite of a place on Copano Bay. The Rangers trapped three Mexican ships in there one time. Used to be a pirate hang-out, too. I say they're headed for Copano or some spot along the shore near there."

"What's it like down thataway?"

"Low ground, lots of live oaks and willows. All that country around Copano Creek is wooded. Maybe I should say it was wooded. I ain't been down there since I helped some Irish folk through that country. The way people keep cuttin' down the trees and mucking out the stumps to make farm-land a body never knows what he'll find when he goes back."

"Maybe that's our chance," Mac suggested, "in that brush and live-oak forest?"

"If we was to ride west we'd come up to Salt Creek. She flows right into that country."

"All right. Let's get going!"

What to *do*? What could they do? Three men against thirty? But it was up to them. Otherwise the girls would be sold as slaves, treated like animals. . . .

They followed Willow Creek until they were within a mile of the wooded region, when they turned at right angles and rode west and south into the trees.

Happy Jack pointed toward some torn-up ground near a bunch of oaks. "Javelinas," he said. "Wild pigs been rooting up the ground for roots an' such. Quite a passel of them."

They followed a dim path into the woods, weaving their way along. The smell of the sea was with them all the time now, mingled here with the smell of decaying vegetation. There was no sound but the hoof-falls of their horses and the sound of leaves brushing their bodies.

"We better find a place to hole up," Jack suggested.

"And if we get those women away we'll need more horses or a wagon."

"No way we'll get a wagon," Dal said.

"Jack? You know this country. Where's Refugio from here?"

"West. Maybe a mite north. It'll be the closest town if we're runnin'."

They found what they wanted in a thick stand of live oak near Copano Creek, a small clearing where there had once been a cabin or barn. The building had been pulled down long ago, but the logs lay about, and part of the roof slanted down until it almost touched the ground. It offered enough shelter for two or three people.

"Better take a stick and stir around in there," Jack warned. "That's a good place for snakes."

Dragging scattered logs into position they made a crude fort and cleared a space to tie the horses. "Get some sleep," Jack advised. "I got an idea we'll be up most of the night."

Happy Jack did not feel happy. He was stiff and tired. This was the most riding he'd done in some time, and he was beginning to feel it.

Dal was pale and tired, not yet recovered from his wound and the weakness with which it left him.

They each found a place to lie down, and stretching out were soon alseep. Later, Mac opened his eyes to see several whooping cranes fly overhead, flying east toward the Gulf. He lay quiet, listening to the snores of Dal and Jack, and then he got up and taking his Spencer, scouted around their hide-out.

No fresh tracks of men or horses. Bear tracks, but several days old, javelinas, and what could be a cat track, a big one, probably a panther. There was no need to worry about them, for once they caught the smell of man they would stay away.

Glancing back, Mac saw both of his companions were still asleep, so he walked into the forest. He was, he felt, not far from Copano. He had been walking for almost an hour when he glimpsed the water. Emerging from the trees, he looked out upon the Gulf. There was no ship.

A few small boats were farther out, but nothing else.

Keeping to the edge of the trees so his body's outline would merge with them, he walked north, scouting for tracks. He found nothing. . . .

Then he heard it. A distant sound of a wagon rolling, bumping over rocks or branches, occasionally a curse from one of the drivers. Two riders came into view, at least three hundred yards off. One stood in his stirrups and looked all around. Mac remained immobile and was not worried. From their distance they would not see him unless he moved. They were well out in the open now, but to cross Copano Creek they would have to turn inland and find a way where the creek was narrower or where crossing was easier.

From the way the sunlight fell, his glasses did not reflect, and he had a chance to study them well. Colonel Ashford still wore his now-shabby uniform coat with the insignia of his rank. There were other faces he could pick out, including that of Frank from the trouble in Victoria.

What could be done to delay them? How could they help the girls to escape? Would there be a chance while crossing the Copano?

Or should they try sharp-shooting, picking off one and then another? He disliked the idea of shooting men from ambush, but they had, in a sense, placed themselves beyond fair play when they took women as prisoners to be sold as slaves.

The shore where they apparently intended going was deserted. Parts of it were cut off from view by low sand-hills piled up by storms in ages past. Hurricanes along this coast struck with frightful effect—that much he knew, although he had never seen one. For a time he had served with a Ranger who had lived on the Gulf Coast and told stories of the storms and the damage they created.

There was no sign of that now. The sky was clear and blue, the air very clear.

Now the caravan had stopped. Several riders had closed in around Ashford and were talking. He wished he could read lips. There had been a man in his outfit who had deaf parents, and had become quite adept at it, learning from them.

They were going to turn. They were going to be coming right toward him, although on the far side of the creek. Bit by bit, so as to offer no decisive, clear-cut movement to be seen, he eased back into the trees, then walked several yards back into the forest.

Retracing his steps he found Happy Jack Traven sitting with a cup of coffee in his hands and Dal tugging on his boots. "Better douse the fire," he said, "but gently. We don't want any smoke."

Dal took up the pot and filled his cup. "Are they coming, Mac?"

"A few miles off. They have to ford Copano Creek

over yonder." He pointed. "There's nothing on the water but a couple of far-off fishing boats. They'll probably make camp on the beach."

"What about that ford?" Happy Jack asked. "If we're goin' to move, it had better be soon."

Mac mentioned his thought about picking them off. "Takes too long," Dal said. "How many could we get before they hole up or fight back? Two? Three?"

Mac filled his own cup from the pot that would soon have to be dumped.

Happy Jack got to his feet. "I'll get the horses, although from what you say they won't be doin' us much good."

Mac stared into the remains of the raked-out fire. Dal was scattering handsful of dirt over the coals. What chance did they have? He stared bitterly, probing his brain for some thought, some idea, some suggestion.

Those girls now, they had to be scared. And what of Susan's mother, who had to leave her little daughter behind, just hoping her father would arrive in time? What must she be thinking now? *Had he come? Suppose he was dead? What would Susan do? What if Indians came first? Had she been wrong? Would it have been better to bring the child along?*

Kate . . . Kate was strong. She was attractive, damned attractive, but she had inner strength and she had grown up on the frontier, using her head every minute.

Yet they would be in despair. After all, by now they must know what lay before them and that a ship was to meet them here.

They could not know that Dal was alive, or perhaps that they were even close. Still, there must have been some talk around their camp. Frank was not the type to keep his mouth shut, so perhaps they did know their brothers were somewhere near.

If so, they would be hoping, and Mac knew that they could not fail them. After all, they were their only chance. "We aren't going to fail," he said aloud, "not if we have to kill every one of them and sink their ship."

Nobody spoke. They felt as he did, but the question was, how?

"When we stampeded the cattle," he said, "that may have given them something to hope on. At least, they knew somebody was around."

"Seen some tracks of wild cattle," Happy Jack remarked. "There's longhorns a-plenty in this brush."

"And about everything else! Everwhere a body looks there's thorns or stickers."

They rinsed their cups at the branch that trickled by under the trees and packed them so they would not rattle.

"Maybe," Dal said, "when they try to ford that creek, we might have a chance."

Mac checked his guns again. His mouth felt dry, and his heart was beating with slow, heavy thumps. What *could* they do? No matter. Now was the time. They had no choice.

"If we could even get one of them away!" Dal said. "Maybe if Jesse—?"

"We don't know what kind of shape he's in. He may be hurt bad. He may be all tied up."

"Leave it to Kate. She won't be tied up, and believe you me, she's got it all figured out by now. If we only knew what she has in mind."

"We'd better leave the horses, and one of us come back for them. It's not easy getting them closer, and one of them might whinny when they smell their stock."

The thicket was tight with interwoven branches and there were places where only a man might get through;

yet as they approached the creek and the Gulf shore
the growth thinned a little, so movement became easier.

Several of the riders were already across the creek
when they arrived. They were sitting their horses, looking back at the approaching caravan. The teams had
been exchanged, and both wagons were now pulled by
oxen from among the captured animals. They were
slower but better for the heavy pulling that might be
expected on the marsh-like banks of the creek and the
heavy sand of the beach.

The supply wagon was first, heavily loaded with both
food and ammunition, as well as bedding. Gingerly, the
oxen came down the marshy bank and into the water. It
was belly deep, but the cattle moved steadily forward.

They were mid-stream when Mac threw his rifle to
his shoulder and shot the lead ox.

The ox threw up its head, then disappeared under
the water. Riders wheeled to face the direction from
which the shot had come. Firing from well back in the
trees, Mac knocked a man from his horse. Happy Jack
got another, and Dal's shot dropped a second ox.

A volley of shots cut through the leaves overhead,
but the Travens had already moved back, keeping low
to the ground.

One of the riders rode his horse into the water to cut
loose the dead oxen. Excited by the smell of blood on
the water the horse began to buck and plunge, throwing its rider into the river.

From the bank of the stream Happy Jack could see
the girls' wagon, but it was surrounded by several riders, and to shoot at them would endanger the girls.

The Travens faded back, deeper into the brush. At
times they had to get down and crawl along game trails,
but they worked their way back.

"We stopped 'em, but now what?" Jack asked.

"They'll send skirmishers into the brush," Mac said, "and we're not apt to get that close again until they're out of the brush."

"There's two less to deal with," Jack said, "and they won't have those oxen cut loose and the wagons out of the way in less than an hour."

It allowed them very little time, and they were no closer to freeing the girls now than before.

Mac seated himself on a log and stared into nothingness. What could they do now? What chance did they have?

Jack's face was a picture of discouragement. Removing his hat he stared into the crown. He looked over at Dal, leaning against a tree.

"Maybe in the sand-hills," Dal said finally. "At least we have an idea where they are going."

Mac got to his feet. "If only that ship doesn't get here. We need time! Time!"

"And that's the one thing we haven't got," Jack said bitterly.

"Tonight," Mac said, "we've got to do something tonight."

NINE

Kate Connery was thinking. Dal was out there. The stories of his death were obviously untrue. Mac was with him, and from a hasty glimpse she had at the stampede she was quite sure the other man was that worthless uncle of Dal's. Well, maybe *worthless* was too strong a word. Yet what could three men do?

They would need help, and if Jesse could get away he could be helping rather than lying on his back and waiting for whatever might happen.

Gretchen and Dulcie would do what they could, which was not much, and besides, she did not want them to draw the anger of their captors. Whatever she did she would do of her own free will, and she was prepared to take the consequences.

Cordelia Atherton . . . she could be depended upon. She was quick, decisive, and unafraid.

"Cordy." She spoke in a low, conversational tone,

but not in a whisper that might draw attention. "We've got to help."

"I've been thinking that."

"They will want to free us, so we must try to foresee what they may do and how we can help."

"There isn't much they can do."

"I know the Travens. They will never stop until we are free or they are dead."

The men were struggling, trying to get the dead ox free from the wagon. The animal was heavy, and it lay under nearly four feet of water, which did not help. The second ox, which was not yet dead, was kicking and threshing around in the water, hampering their efforts.

Colonel Ashford returned, riding up to the bank. With several others he had ridden ahead to scout the trail just before the attack. He sat his horse, watching the men clearing the dead ox from the yoke and trying to drag it free.

"Get both of them out on the bank and butcher them," he said. "We will need the meat."

"We lost two men," somebody said. "Farrow's gone, and so is Johnson."

Ashford swore under his breath. Two good men, and Farrow had been a solid, dependable man, not like some of those who followed him.

"Butler," he said, "take two men and bury them. On the bank somewhere. Keep their guns and catch up their horses. We'll need them."

"What use will horses be on a ship?" Frank asked.

"We aren't on a ship yet," Ashford replied brusquely.

By the time they got the two oxen from the water and butchered them, more than two hours had been lost. The air had grown heavy, and it was very hot. In the distance there was a roll of thunder.

Kate rested her elbows on her knees and stared out of the back end of the wagon. Happy Jack Traven! That was the uncle, and he was not really worthless, simply a man who liked trouble or seemed to. Unless she was mistaken, there would be a storm, and a storm offered opportunities. But first she had to think. At all costs they must not be put aboard a ship. Once they were at sea, the Travens would have no chance.

It might have been the idea of the storm, but it was more than likely the ship and Dal's uncle Jack, that made her think of her own uncle.

She had seen him but once, when she was a small girl, and she clearly remembered him. He was her father's older brother, a former sea captain who had swallowed the anchor, as the saying was, and gone ashore and to ranching. He was not the only one, for Captain Richard King who founded the King Ranch had been a steamboat captain before he began ranching.

Martin Connery held himself aloof from his family and lived surrounded by retainers, most of them members of his old crew or seamen he had known, now turned cowboys. He had been master of a privateer and often suspected of piracy, and he tolerated no nonsense from anyone.

She had never visited his ranch but knew its approximate location. It could not be far away.

Suddenly, the wagon gave a lurch, there was a sloshing of water and much cursing, and then the wagon moved and a few minutes later tilted sharply back as the oxen pulled it up the bank and out of the water.

Kate peered outside. The sky was heavily overcast now. It was going to blow, and she knew storms along the Gulf Coast often reached hurricane proportions. She thought of the broken glass from the bottle she had found. She had hidden several pieces of the glass in the wagon. Now she got out a piece of it and moved closer to Jesse.

She could see his eyes in the semi-darkness, and she touched his shoulder warningly and then went to work with the sharp edge of the broken glass to cut the rawhide that bound his ankles.

Suddenly the canvas at the end of the wagon was jerked back. It was Colonel Ashford. She had barely time to let the fragment of glass drop to the canvas that covered the wagon's floor.

"Are you all right?" He looked from one to the other, his eyes sharp and suspicious.

"We aren't complaining," Cordelia replied, "although we'd be happier at home."

Kate saw his eyes on her and was well aware of his interest. She smiled a little and said, "When you have time, we must talk."

"It could be now," Ashford said. "We're making coffee."

He helped her from the back of the wagon, and when she was on the ground she smoothed her dress, then touched a hand to her hair.

"You must have planned all this very hurriedly," she said.

He gave her all his attention. "Why do you say that?"

"Because it is unlike you to be so foolish. By kidnapping us you will have aroused people all across the country. They may be slow to act, but they will act, and you will never dare come this way again.

"It seemed to me that you were in a hurry to succeed in what you planned, and much of what happened was simply a matter of doing what could be done at the moment. I believe a man as clever as you obviously are would have planned more carefully."

"The surrender of Lee was unexpected," he agreed.

"Of course. Stealing women is one way of arousing a country against you, and by now men are moving. There will be a dozen armed bands on your trail by now."

"And soon we will be aboard ship and gone," he said, smiling.

"Perhaps. What if your ship does not come? I have helped to fight Comanches, Colonel Ashford, and one thing I would not wish is to be caught on an open beach in a fight with men who could fire from the protection of sand hills."

"As I said, we will be aboard ship."

"Have you looked at the weather? No ship is going to want to try those narrow inlets from the sea during a storm. It might be a week before a ship can drop anchor out here, and by that time it will be too late."

"You are an intelligent young woman."

"You knew that all along, and you should have talked to me before all this happened. For example you are going all the way to Mexico to get arms, money, and horses. I could have told you where they could be had much easier."

Ashford looked out toward the Gulf. The water looked dark and ugly. "Why are you telling me this?"

"I am a Confederate, too. You never asked any questions. You just grabbed us and ran. I did not like Lee's surrender, either, and I think victory can still be had."

"There was no time for questions, no time for planning. We had to move. Above all, I had to keep my men busy to retain their loyalty."

"And now?"

He paused, considering it. This young woman made a lot of sense. He had moved fast, too fast for planning. He had to deal the cards, and there had been no time to stack the deck.

"What would you have done?" his eyes searched hers. "You spoke of guns, horses, and money?"

"Just south of here," she said, "I have an uncle named Martin Connery. He is," and she had no idea whether what she said was true or not, "a confirmed Confederate, but more than that, he likes to make money. If he was approached in the right way . . ."

"Do you think he would help us?"

"I can promise nothing, but if you go to him, go quietly. Ask that he help, or suggest that he help. He has thousands of horses and he has cattle. His ranch is out of the way south of here, and he has few visitors. Yet he could gather and equip an army."

"Martin Connery, you said? I seem to know the name?"

"You may have heard it. As a boy in his teens he fought with a Kentucky contingent at San Jacinto."

"And you think he would help us?"

"I am sure of it, if you approach him in the right way." She paused and lied in her teeth. "I was his favorite niece. If you had come to me in the beginning . . ."

"Perhaps that was a mistake. How far away is this uncle of yours?"

"Just south of here, near Mission Bay."

He turned away. "I shall give it some thought. Your idea may be a good one." His eyes searched hers. "Why should you do this?"

"I told you. I am a Confederate. I was sick when I heard of Lee's surrender. Besides," she paused and let some of her smile creep into her eyes, "I like a man of action. I like a man who does things. Of course, you were under duress, and it is not always possible to think clearly."

"This uncle of yours. You would go to him with me?"

"Of course."

He walked away, and after a moment she got back into the wagon, her heart beating slowly and heavily. Now with a little luck . . .

"Kate, how could you lie like that?" Dulcie protested. "You know Uncle Martin has never come near us. He does not like us, and I don't think he cared who won the War. I know he was not a Confederate, and he did not believe they had a chance to win. Papa told us he always said all the arms factories were in the North. Besides, he's a mean, cruel old man!"

"Maybe he is, but he's kin." And after a minute, Kate added, "And he's very smart. I just hope he's not only shrewd enough but willing to help."

"Why should he?"

Of course, there was no reason why he should. Simply none at all. Her father had seen him only twice in many years, and the meetings had not been friendly. He was a hard, cruel old man, and even if he had not been a pirate, he acted like one.

Feeling around in the bottom of the wagon, she retrieved the bit of glass and went to work on Jesse's rawhide ropes again. They were thick and tightly woven, part of an old lariat, she believed.

There was a brief spatter of rain. The wagons were moving again.

"He should stay in the edge of the woods," Dulcie said. "If he goes to the shore now, he's crazy!"

"Jesse? How are you feeling?"

"Much better. If I could get loose . . ."

"Run for it. Hide. Find Dal and Mac. Tell them I am going to take Ashford to Uncle Martin if I can."

"You've got to be crazy! He won't help! You know your Uncle Martin. He wouldn't help anybody! And he never had any use for your pa. You know that. He's a scoundrel!"

"Then he's probably just what is needed to cope with Colonel Ashford."

What *had* she been thinking of? Martin Connery cared for nobody. He was tough and mean, and he would not help. But she was sure he would not like Ashford, either. Martin Connery despised causes and those who fought for them. He fought for himself and perhaps the men who served him. He had no loyalty to her father, herself, or anybody else.

He had been a famous duellist and had killed a number of men in duels both here and abroad, several of them in New Orleans and Charleston. He was also famous as a womanizer.

Yet it might delay the moment when they were taken aboard ship, and something might happen to save them.

The wind came with a rush. The wagon rocked on its wheels, and the canvas pushed in. Frightened, the girls clung together. Much more of this and the wagon would be blown over.

Jesse sat up and held his wrists out to Kate. "It's now or never," he said. *"Hurry!"*

Desperately she sawed at the already partly cut rawhide. Above the roar of the sea, the crashing of thunder, and the pounding of the rain she could hear the strangled sound of voices, of men shouting to each other. Soon that was stilled. No doubt they had taken cover.

The rawhide parted suddenly, and Jesse took the broken glass from Kate and went to work on the bonds on his ankles. A moment, and he was free. He chafed his wrists and ankles.

"They will be out in the woods somewhere," she said.

"I'll have to be lucky. There won't be any tracks."

She had not thought of that. Of course there wouldn't

be. The rain was falling in sheets. At the back of the wagon, Jesse peered out, hesitated a moment, and was gone like a shadow. One moment he was there, and then he was gone.

Quickly she drew the laces together and tied the canvas as tightly as she could. Straining her ears, she heard no sound but the roaring of the wind and the sea. She huddled with the others, frightened as they were that the wagon might tip over.

Suppose . . . just suppose they all tried it? Suppose they went now, suddenly, running into the forest? They'd be drenched to the skin within minutes, and in their heavy clothes they would not be able to move swiftly enough, yet . . .

Quickly, she went to the back of the wagon. She started to unfasten the laces when a rough voice said, "Just you set back an' set tight, ma'am. Ain't nobody goin' no place!"

Too late! In the confusion of the storm they had been forgotten, an oversight now taken care of.

She moved away. Had Jesse made it? Or was he lying out there now, stabbed or bayoneted to death, lying in the mud and slush, breathing his last?

It had been a good thought, but it had come too late. And just as well they had not gone with Jesse, for they would only have been an encumbrance, slowing him down until he, too, was taken or killed.

They could only wait. . . .

TEN

For one moment after his feet hit the ground, Jesse took a quick look around.

Nobody was in sight. There were only the two wagons, the horses standing heads down in the driving rain, and a few scattered tracks showing where the men had fled for shelter in that first, fierce thrust of the storm. On the edge of the forest several trees had been blown down in a bygone storm, and their trunks had been covered by debris, forming a natural shed that offered at least partial shelter.

The one look was all he needed. Jesse plunged into the forest, ran desperately hard, tripped over a root, and fell sprawling into the mud and leaves. Scrambling up, he took a hasty look around.

A man was moving toward the wagon from which he had just come! Jesse ran into the forest, ducking and dodging among the trees, his face lashed by blown

branches and whipped by the driving rain. He fell
again, got up again, glimpsed what seemed to be an
opening and dove into it, running hard.

Distance . . . distance was what he needed now.
After that he could stop and look for a place to hide.

Where would Dal be, and Mac? Had they found
shelter, or were they out in the storm?

He ran until he was gasping for breath, then fell
against a tree, almost strangled by blown rain. He clung
to the tree, then ran on. Time and again he fell, sometimes tripping, sometimes slipping. Weaving among the
trees as he must he could not tell how far he had
come.

This was snake country, but he need not fear them
for they would have been smart enough to find shelter
before this storm hit. As he ran, his mind began to
work. The first blind panic gone, he tried to think, to
decide what he must do, where he must look for his
brothers.

Running as he had, the thought came to mind of an
old argument he and his brothers had often debated,
whether one ran because he was afraid or was afraid
because he ran. For running contributed to fear, he was
sure of that now. Deliberately, he forced himself to
slow down, to look, to see where he was going.

He needed to find his brothers, but he also needed
shelter, a place to hide, and weapons of some kind. The
forest offered nothing beyond a club or a sharp stick,
but there were plenty of both. Wind whipped the trees,
and the driving rain continued. If he stopped to catch a
breath he ended with a mouth full of water.

He stopped, leaned against a huge old cypress, and
tried to rest a moment.

Escaping had been his only chance. As long as he

remained with the girls there was no way in which he could help, and once they examined him again they would discover he was no longer badly hurt and could be imprisoned somewhere away from the girls. Now that he was free he must do what he could.

His brothers would not be far away. They would be within striking distance of the wagons, and probably where they could easily come within watching distance of the route the caravan would take when it started for the beach.

He tried to orient himself. He had run west, he believed, away from the shore, and although he had twisted and turned his general direction had been west. So what he must now do was to turn north or south and try to discover their hiding place. South would be best, for that was the direction in which the wagons would be moving.

If only he had a gun! Or even a knife with which to cut something, to form some kind of a weapon. He could make a bow and arrow. He had often made crude ones as a child, but they had been used to kill small animals when hunting. He could build one now that had greater power. But it would take time, more time than he was likely to have.

Once it was discovered that he had escaped, would they come hunting him? It was possible, but doubtful. There was an urgency about those men, a need to push on, to get something done, to meet their ship.

Wiping the streaming water from his eyes, he looked around, then turned left and started walking into the woods. He kept stumbling and slipping, for the earth was soggy with rain, and there were many exposed roots and fallen trees.

He was, he realized suddenly, desperately tired. His

wound had caused loss of blood, and he had not regained his strength. Before he went much further, he must think of rest, of a place to hole up and shelter himself.

He stumbled on, pausing to lean against a tree from time to time to choose his way. He was very weak. He had not realized how weak, for lying in the wagon there had been no way to test his strength or stamina. Yet he was free, for the moment at least, and he must find his brothers and some way to help the girls.

Lightning flashed, and there was a crash of thunder. He believed he could see a partial track, the indentation of a boot heel. He started in the direction indicated.

Mac and Dal were both tall men, and each had a good stride. So allowing for that he began to search for further tracks and after a few minutes found what appeared to be a track, although it was almost erased by the rain. Pushing on, he walked for some distance and was in despair over losing the trail when he saw another track, clearly defined and probably less than a half hour old.

They would not continue in this storm but would find a shelter somewhere or build one. In this forest it would be simple to build a shelter and then cover the muddy earth with boughs. . . .

He saw the bars of a corral first, then a shed, and beyond it, a tumbled-down log cabin.

He hesitated, wary of a trap. The rain had eased for the moment, and he crouched, watching the cabin intently. He heard a horse blow. Swiftly, he moved to another tree, putting the shed between himself and the cabin. Then he ducked between the poles of the old corral and came up to the shed and peered between the logs.

The first horse was Bonnie Prince, the horse Dal had ridden away to war.

They were here then, but he must approach with caution. Who else might be there he did not know, nor whether they were free or prisoners, or even if they were not here at all and the horse had merely been stolen.

His brothers were quick to shoot, but he was not worried about that. He knew them too well. They would never shoot at anything they could not identify.

Waiting just an instant longer, he dashed for the corner of the cabin and paused, flattened out against it. From inside he heard Dal speaking.

"Playin' games again, I guess. I don't know why he'd be standin' out there in the rain when it's dry in here. You reckon them Yankees knocked his brains out or somethin'?"

Jesse walked around the corner of the house and into the door, which stood open.

They had a small fire going in the fire-place and a coffee-pot on the coals.

Dal was squatting beside the fire. Mac was seated on a bench nearby, and Happy Jack was stretched out on the flat boards of a corner bed. The cabin was old, long abandoned, and barely hanging together, but the roof was intact and it was dry.

Dal passed him a cup of coffee, and Mac threw a blanket over his shoulders. Between sips of coffee, he explained what happened.

"How are the girls?" Dal asked.

"Good as could be expected. That Atherton woman is game. She's cool and she's thinkin' all the while, and of course, you know Kate."

"What about Kate?" Dal asked.

Jesse sipped coffee and told them about Martin Connery. Dal swore as he listened, muttering under his breath. "Martin Connery? The man's a bloody pirate! He wasn't on speakin' terms with any of the family."

Happy Jack got up and came over to the fire. "Look here, boy, you'd better get some sleep. You look kinda caved in. We're not goin' to move out of here until daylight, anyway."

As Jesse went to the bed and fell on it, Jack squatted on his heels. "That Kate, now—there's a thinkin' woman. If she can talk Ashford into goin' to Connery she's maybe done the smartest thing she could do."

"Him? Martin Connery's a thief! The old devil stole a Navy pinnace right out of the harbor at Kingston, sailed her away right under the eyes of the Navy!

"He'll stop at nothing to make a dollar. The last year he was at sea they say he flew the flag of Chile, had a Letter of Marque from them, or something. And it was said he took forty prizes.

"Several different countries had ships out hunting him, so he ups and disappears. Seemed to drop right off the edge of the world, but he done no such thing. He come here to Texas, bought him a ranch, and hid his ship in Mission Bay. He knew every hide-out along the coast, and he always kept to shallow-draft ships that could sail in less water than it would take to float a tea-cup, so nobody could foller where he went."

"They find him?" Mac asked.

"Never did. If they'd have found him they'd have hung him, but while they are scouring the seas hunting him, he's ranching in Texas, cool as you please."

"Was he a Confederate sympathizer?"

"Him? He never did anything unless it paid him. He scoffed at the South. He seemed to like Southern folks and their ways, but he thought they were foolish to go to war. I hear he did some blockade runnin', but who knows?"

Mac looked at Happy Jack. "Why do you think Kate did a good thing in tryin' to get them together?"

"Look at it. Martin Connery could steal the suspenders off Ashford's shoulders without him knowing they were gone. He'll see right through Ashford.

"Ashford may talk like a patriot, and he may even think he is, but actually the man's a thief and a highbinder, only he isn't in Martin Connery's class.

"Connery will see right through him, and Ashford will be lucky to get away with his pants. You just wait an' see. Ashford's using his loyalty to the Confederacy as an excuse to steal and cheat. What kind of a man would sell decent women into slavery? Connery's a fighter and a pirate, but there was never anything penny-ante about him. He laid it on the line and played the cards he was dealt, and off the bottom of the deck if he was doing the dealing."

One by one they rolled in their blankets and slept while the rain fell unceasing. Wind worried around the eaves, rattled a broken branch across the shingles, and blew rain in the broken door, which had been merely propped in place.

Out in the forest a tree, weakened by years of buffeting, finally collapsed and fell. The sound disturbed no one.

Only when the first daylight came did they open their eyes. Mac slipped out of his blankets and started a fire, shoving the coffee-pot close to the coals and adding water.

Tip-toeing to the door, he peered out. It was still raining, but scarcely more than a drizzle now. The door of the stable was still closed. Nonetheless, he felt uneasy. Returning to the fire he tugged on his boots and slung his belt around his hips with the holster containing the Remington.

Dipping up some water with a gourd dipper, he emptied it into an old wash-pan and bathed his face and hands, drying them on his shirt, which he then put on.

Again he went to the door. "Dal?" he spoke over his shoulder. "Better get movin'. I've got an uneasy feelin'."

Happy Jack walked to the fire and tugged on his boots. "Coffee smells good. You checked the horses?"

"I'm going to saddle up now." He donned his coat and took up the Spencer .52, slinging the Quick-Loader over his shoulder.

The limited supplies they had brought along on the spare horse from the Atherton place were nearly gone, so they split the remainder into four packs, and Jesse rigged a saddle from some blankets and straps.

The rain had eased somewhat, but the earth was soggy, and the trees dripped heavy drops into the muck below. Mac thrust his spare pistol behind his belt, eyes busy on the trees.

The situation worried him. He did not like remaining too long in one place, for fear of discovery. Their smoke was unlikely to be seen in the rain, yet there was the chance.

Mounting up, Mac led the way through the trees toward the south. Happy Jack closed up on him and riding abreast said, "We've got to watch ourselves. There's a peninsula runs out into the bay somewhere along here, and if we get out on it we're stuck."

The rain ceased falling, and there was no sound in the woods but that of their horses' hoofs. Mac tried to think ahead, to find an opening, a chance to rescue the girls without getting themselves killed. If anything happened to them, the girls would be condemned to a life of misery and cruelty.

Suppose Ashford swallowed the bait Kate had offered? Suppose he left his wagons and most of his men and rode south to Martin Connery's ranch? He would certainly take Kate with him, but the others would be left behind. Yet could Ashford trust his men to leave the girls alone in his absence?

How many men would he take with him, leaving how many behind?

Happy Jack had fallen back, as it was strictly a single-file trail. Now he called in a low voice.

"Mac? The brush is thinnin' out! Ride careful!"

Mac drew up, and when they stopped they listened. A faint yell came to them, then a whip-crack, almost like a pistol shot in the silence after the storm. Mac waited, watching and listening, not daring to move lest their movement be detected. Beyond the trees and brush, thin in places, could be seen the shadowy movements of the caravan wending its way across a wide open space leading to the beach.

Mac used his glass. Ashford was still with them, riding well out in front with four other men. These Mac studied, as one of them might well be the second in command, who must be dealt with.

"Jack? How far away is Connery's place?"

"Ain't more'n ten mile, I'd say. Maybe less. Right ahead of us there's a bay, round as the moon. They call it one thing or another; mostly nowadays its called Mission Bay. Martin Connery's place is just beyond. He keeps a schooner anchored in the bay in case he has to get away to sea again."

If that was true, then the chances were that Ashford

would go into camp on the beach and wait for the ship he expected, and he might seize the chance to ride south and see Martin Connery.

"They're stoppin'," Jesse said. "I see the girls gettin' out."

ELEVEN

When the wagons stopped, Kate Connery peered out to see a wide white beach sloping very slightly toward the Gulf. She had only the vaguest idea of where she was and was totally unfamiliar with the area. Martin Connery lived somewhere to the south, how far she was not sure.

She had seen her uncle but once, when she was a small girl, and she remembered him only as a somewhat frightening but romantic figure of a man who gave orders like a cracking whip and tolerated no disobedience, or even hesitation.

He had about him an air of command, and he strode like he was walking his own quarter-deck.

The man named Butler came by and scratched on the canvas. "You can get out if you like," he said. "Stretch your legs a mite. Looks like we might be here quite a spell."

"Thank you." Butler was a man of thirty-five, and there was about him a sense of one who had seen better times and who knew how to conduct himself. "When you make some coffee might we have some?"

"Certainly, ma'am, I shall see to it."

He walked his horse away, and one by one they got down from the wagon. Across the neck of the bay on which they were, loomed another shore, perhaps two or three miles away. It was a low shore with a few scattered trees.

"Stay close to the wagon," Kate advised.

"Can't we go down to the water? I'd like to wash my hands," Gretchen asked.

"Wait. Maybe they will let us, but the less attention we attract the better."

"I wonder where the boys are?" Dulcie asked.

"Jesse got away, at least," Kate said. "I think they were glad to be rid of him."

"Do you suppose he will find them?"

"Of course."

Yet she was not all that sure. How could he find them in all the wet forest? How far could he travel, weak as he was and without a horse?

For all she knew Jesse might be . . . out there in the forest now, dead or dying. He seemed to have gotten away, but how could they be sure? If one of these men killed him he might not even comment on it. They had already shown themselves to be very casual about killing, and she was beginning to believe that under his facade Ashford was as bad as the others. He considered himself a patriot and a gentleman, but what kind of a gentleman would kidnap young girls and plan to sell them into slavery? Yet as long as he wore the cloak of a gentleman he might behave like one, and without him they had nothing.

Butler? She did not know about Butler. Would he help? Was he too loyal to Ashford or to the Cause? Or would he take the risk of helping them escape?

Escape to where? Where could they go? They were miles and miles from home, and they were out on a flat white beach with only a tangle of forest and undergrowth behind the beach. There was no place to which they could run, nobody to ask for help.

Martin Connery? Her feeling was that Connery would have nothing but contempt for Ashford, but she wasn't sure. Nor did she know how many men he had or whether he would try to help her.

Why should he? He had never seemed to care for his family, and certainly none of them cared for him. He was, to their thinking, a black sheep. He had strayed from the fold, and as far as the family was concerned he could stay there.

Yet . . .

It was a forlorn hope but the only one she had. That and whatever the boys might do.

The sun was warm, and the glare off the sand caused them to squint. Two men sat out on the beach between them and the water, rifles across their knees. Some others had taken the horses and oxen and were leading them toward some grass at the edge of the trees. Several cooking fires had been started, and she could smell coffee.

Ashford was coming toward her.

She got up, brushing off her dress, putting a strand of hair in place. He stopped before her, feet apart, staring. "You're quite a woman, Kate, and you've got brains, too. We'd make a team, you and I."

"I am not a soldier."

He chuckled. "Of course not, but you have brains."

The smile left his face. "This uncle of yours? He was a Southern sympathizer?"

"I am sure that was where his sympathies lay." Then to offer something more to Ashford's taste, she added, "He was, I believe, a blockade runner."

"Ah?"

It was a wild card she was playing, a pitiful gamble against impossible odds. Martin Connery had never shown the slightest interest in any of his family, and there was no reason why he should now. By leading these renegades to him she might be endangering his life, but somehow, some way, she must save the girls from what lay before them.

What she was offering Ashford was the chance of an alliance, and if that failed, the prospect of loot. That he was considering both possibilities she was sure, and if she remembered her uncle correctly he was perfectly capable of handling Ashford.

What right had she to risk her uncle's life to save herself and the others? Exactly none at all. But there was no alternative.

Ashford stared out over the bay, considering. She had, she believed, detected some uneasiness in him, perhaps about the expected ship. Was its arrival uncertain? Or did he not trust those with whom he would be dealing? At least, she had offered another possibility.

"Colonel Ashford? The girls would like to bathe their hands and feet. Might we go to the water?"

"Of course. But no tricks, understand? And please, offer my men no temptations. Discipline is a delicate matter now that the War is over. We must tread carefully." Then he smiled. "If temptation is offered, let it be to me. I can handle it better."

"Thank you." She walked to the girls and explained. Ashford called to the guards and told them to allow the girls to go to the edge of the water, no farther. And no straying to right or left.

When they were at the water's edge and had washed a bit she gathered them together on the sand, out of hearing of the guards. Carefully, she explained what she had done, clarifying points that might have been left unclear.

"So he may want me to ride away with him, to go to visit Uncle Martin. . . ."

"Mother always said he was a devil," Dulcie insisted.

"At least he's our devil, or I hope he is. What other chance do we have? The boys may be able to help us, but they are so few, and what can they do?"

"When will you go?"

"I've no idea. He may decide not to go, and we might go at once. There's something he does not like about the ship that is coming in. Perhaps he doesn't trust those on the ship."

"I wish Mac and Dal would come," Gretchen said. "I'm so tired of all this! I want to go *home*!"

"We all do, but there's no help for it now."

"But why did it happen to us?" Gretchen was near tears.

"We were in the way, there's no other answer. I doubt they had any such plans, but then riding south they decided to raid your ranch, and there we were. They may be thinking of selling us into slavery, but they may change their minds and do whatever they wish to do right here. We have to be prepared for that. But remember—the boys are out there in the woods, and some one of them is watching, you can be sure of that. If the worst comes they would come in shooting, you can be sure of it."

"They'd be killed!"

"I think they are prepared to run that risk. We will just have to wait."

Under the glaring sun the beach was hot and white, the sky overhead a misty blue, misty with rising heat. Turning from where they were seated on the sand they could look back at the wagons, stark and still against the skyline.

Kate knew she must keep cool, she must think, think, *think*! Somewhere there was an answer. There had to be.

"I wonder where the boys are?" Dulcie said. "I wonder where they are right now?"

Mac lay on his belly on a low sand-hill covered with stunted brush. It was an unlikely place for a man to hide, but good for that very reason. What he needed was a good view of Ashford's camp, such as it was.

They had simply drawn up their wagons on the sand and corralled the horses close by. The oxen had been led out on the grass no more than sixty yards from where Mac lay.

There were seven girls and women down there, Mac thought, Kate, Dulcie, Gretchen, Mrs. Atherton, and three whom he did not know. They had walked down to the edge of the water now and were bathing their hands and feet and faces. Several were making an effort to comb their hair, which had become tangled and messy. Kate was sitting with the Atherton woman. At least, he guessed it was she. The age was about right.

There were two guards on the beach about thirty yards from the girls. There were several other men gathered around a blanket, playing cards. A couple who were probably cooks were preparing food. He counted fifteen men . . . there should be more.

Had some eluded him? Were they out in the woods now, trying to track down the Travens? There had been times, of course, when their observation of the Ashford group had been less than perfect. Occasionally during the storm they had been hiding out or seeking shelter, and they had to prepare food from time to time.

Well, Mac reflected, until something happened, that chore would bother them no longer. Their limited supplies were gone except for a smidgeon of coffee.

The nearest town was probably Refugio, but whatever happened here would happen soon, and they dared not risk letting one man ride into town and back, which could take the better part of a day.

Mac, watching the men before him, trying to get a count, had reached his position too late to see Sam Hall go into the brush.

Sam was a big, burly man, and he was collecting wood for the cooking fires. He had gathered an armful of dry wood and was walking back, following a game trail toward the shore, when he saw a boot-track, and it was fresh.

The track was obviously made since the rain, and a blade of grass was just rising from where it had been crushed down. Sam knew that might take minutes, but not much longer. Probably less than an hour, more likely less than half that time. Sam Hall put down his armful of wood, taking great care to make no sound.

When the wood was on the sand he straightened very slowly. He was within a hundred yards of the wagons. Whoever had made that track had to be very close. Ashford had been worried about the Travens. Well, in less than a minute there'd be one less.

Sam Hall had come from Ohio, was wanted there for murder, and had fled to the South and joined the Army. He was a man to whom killing and violence came naturally. Had it been left to him they'd have had those women long since, and they'd never have wasted time carting that wounded Jesse Traven around. He'd have knocked him in the head when caught. No use wasting a bullet.

He was prepared to use one now, and to not waste it. Lifting the flap of his holster without making a sound, he drew his pistol. He wanted to ease back the hammer but decided against it. The click might warn the man he was hunting.

Suppose there was more than one? Well, he had seen but one track, and it was unlikely there'd be more this close. Also, he was going to start shooting before anyone saw him. He would have the advantage.

Sam was in thick brush, only the narrow trail winding through it. Directly before him was a dead tree trunk, the bark falling away from it, and some thirty yards further on was a low hummock of sand covered with brush. That was it, that was where Traven would be hiding.

He took a careful step, then another. He was sweating. The sun was hot, of course. He mopped his brow with the hand holding the pistol, and light glinted from the barrel.

Mac Traven, lying in the brush, caught a faint flicker of that movement but was not alarmed. It could have been a drop of rain still clinging to a leaf. It could have been . . .

Sam Hall stepped over the log, putting his foot down carefully. As he did so he saw Mac Traven not twenty feet away, lying on his belly in the sand. He lifted his pistol and let the weight down on the boot that had stepped over the log. Under the sand and out of sight was a small branch. As his weight came down the branch broke and Mac Traven whipped around like a cat. Sam Hall's gun was up and the hammer coming back when something struck him a wicked blow in the chest, and then he heard a gun-shot.

Sam Hall took a half step back as his own gun went off, kicking sand three feet from Traven, who was coming toward him. Sam tried to lift his pistol again but his fingers were numb.

As Traven came face to face with him he felt the pistol slip from his hand. He said, "I guess you hit me."

"I guess I did," Mac said, and went by him, ducking into the brush. Within minutes there would be men all over, hunting him.

Under the shelter of the trees, he glanced back. Men were coming, but the one he had shot was still standing there. As he looked, the man fell.

Sam Hall's face was in the sand. He was choking, but not on sand. He tried to cough, and blood spilled over his chin. He struggled to sit up as men swarmed around him.

"Sam! Sam? What happened?"

"Ohio," Sam Hall muttered, "I always figured on goin' back. By this time they'd have forgot that man I . . ."

He leaned forward, head hanging, hands on his knees.

"Sam . . . ?"

Butler touched his shoulder. "Sam?"

Sam Hall turned over into the sand. Frank looked down at him, then commented, "Wherever he's gone, Butt, it ain't Ohio. I'd bet you on that."

TWELVE

The tall gray-haired man accepted the drink and dropped into the big hide-bound chair. "It was several days ago," he said, "in Victoria. But it bothered me, so I rode over. I had an idea you ought to know."

"Three of them, you say?"

"Right. The only name I got was of the man I spoke of. He told them his name was Major Mac Traven, and he said it like he expected it to mean something.

"Tall man, tall as you, I'd say, and broad in the shoulder. Very cool. Neatest thing I ever saw the way he dropped those sacks. No way the man could avoid falling, and when he looked up, Traven was holding a gun.

"My impression was that although he was not looking for trouble he was a man who could handle it. He gave them a warning and then left town."

Martin Connery strode across the room and dropped

into a similar chair. He tasted the rum and lemon in his glass. "Thirty men, you say? Renegades, probably. And this man Traven, he said they had captive women? I wonder what Traven's interest was?"

"My hunch was that some of them were kin to him. I don't recall whether he said as much or not, but that was my impression. And they were headed south."

The gray-haired man looked into his glass. "Captain, I don't like to say this, but you know as well as I do that when there's trouble down here, people look to you. I mean, they believe you're involved."

"I'm not involved in this."

"The man said his name was Traven."

"Hell, Nick, I'm not responsible for everybody. I don't know of any Traven."

He paused. "Come to think of it I do have some kin-folk somewhere north and west of here. I met them but once or twice and then stayed clear of them. They didn't like me, and I just didn't want any kin-folk around. I've had troubles enough."

They sat silent. A big grandfather's clock ticked loudly. "You've got to understand. The Connerys always regarded me as the black sheep of the family. They were solid, church-going folk, hard-working and pioneering most of the time. Every time one of them seems to get to where he could have a decent living he picks up and goes further west.

"As for the Travens, we've no connection I know of except that I heard one of the Connery girls was sweet on a Traven. I don't know how I came to mention it to you. It wasn't that important, actually." He paused, sipped his drink, and said, "You've a good memory, Nick. That must have been years ago."

"It's an unusual name." Nick got out a cigar. "Captain, we've been friends for years now, but aside from that, you represent a lot of my business. I wouldn't want anything to happen to you, and that's a tough lot of men."

Martin Connery gave him a thin smile. "I've some tough men, too."

"But you were unwarned, unaware. Now you are alerted." Nick got to his feet. "I've business in Refugio, and then I'll be riding back to Victoria."

He paused. "Captain? Give it some thought. Why would such an outfit be coming down *here*? If they were escaping over the border, as some of the Confederates have been doing, there are more direct routes. I believe the answer can be but one of two things. Raiding or meeting a ship."

"I've been thinking of that."

"Slavers used to land contraband slaves on Copano Bay. You know that, and I do. Many a time when Lafitte couldn't get them to New Orleans through the bayous they were landed here. In fact, he used this for a rendezvous after he was driven off Galveston Island."

"It was one of his men who piloted me in here the first time," Connery said.

"Captain? Those kin-folk of yours up north? There were young women in the lot, right?"

Connery took his glass from his mouth. He swore suddenly, bitterly. "Of course there were! She was a little girl then, but by now she'd be a young woman. There might be others. I don't know. Still, that's highly unlikely that something like you describe could happen. They were conservative people and I imagine would be fairly well off."

"It can happen to anyone. Think of it. If the women were in the way and this renegade outfit was riding through?"

After Nick Chandler had gone, Captain Martin

Connery walked to the side-board and placed the glasses there.

A slender Chinese came in. "Anything else, sir?"

"Yes, there is. Ask Ephraim to step in, will you?"

He walked back and dropped into his chair. It was unlikely, but Nick was right when he thought such a group could spell trouble. They would be living off the country, but they were not going to live off his cattle nor steal his horses. If they wanted to go to Mexico they could keep right on going. He wanted no trouble.

Ephraim Calder was a man almost as wide as he was tall, but he carried no fat. He was broad, thick, and powerfully muscled, and he had served with Connery for twenty years.

"Eph, I want you to have three men scout the country north of here. Send some men who can keep out of sight and out of trouble. I want to know what is going on."

Quickly, he sketched in what had happened and what he believed.

"Captain, one of our men who was riding along the north side of the bay heard a shot. Two shots he believed, close together. He was several miles out from the bay, hunting strays."

"All right, sentries and scouts, armed and ready. We don't know what may happen."

"Yes, sir." Ephraim stopped at the door and turning, smiled at Connery. "Almost like the old days, eh Cap'n?"

When Ephraim had gone, Martin Connery walked to his desk and took out a pistol, a Remington Navy. He balanced it in his hands for a moment, liking the feel of it, then thrust it behind his belt and out of sight behind the short jacket he wore.

From another drawer he took a carefully drawn map of the shore-line covering the area from Tres Paglacios

Bay to Corpus Christi, studying it with care. It was an area he had ridden over countless times, and he had sailed along the coast almost as often. Yet he wanted a refreshing glimpse of it. Seeing a situation on a map was much different from being over the ground in person. Neither should exclude the other.

The map gave one perspective, the over-all view, while being on the ground itself gave one an immediate knowledge of terrain, plant life, obstructions, and whatever else might be encountered.

He added a bit more lemon to his rum and returned to his chair. That niece of his . . . what was her name?

Kate . . . that was it. Katherine, of course, but they had called her Kate, a feisty little thing with big eyes.

That fellow now? Colonel Ashford, was it? What would he be wanting? To meet a ship, no doubt some gun-runner or slave-ship. A lot of the old illicit slave traders had haunted this harbor in years gone by. He would have no part of that. Had he been active in the days when it was legal, he still would have taken no part in dealing with slaves. And the importation of slaves into the United States had ended, legally, in 1808.

To meet a ship, perhaps, but primarily he would be looking for loot. Lonely ranches close to the sea had always been vulnerable. He himself had often sailed in close and dropped his hook long enough to steal a few head of cattle or sheep for food aboard ship.

Thirty men? He had half that many, but Connery knew what he had and was not worried.

He was at breakfast on the terrace at dawn when a rider rode in and talked to Ephraim Calder. Then both approached him. He sliced a bit from his melon and listened.

Two wagons were drawn up on the sand this side of Copano Creek. There had been some shooting, and

through a spy-glass his man had seen them burying a
man.

"One less," he commented.

"But now ten of them are approaching. They left
camp shortly before daybreak and should be here by
noon-time. There is one woman among them. She rides
beside he who is their leader."

"Very well. When they arrive you may bring four of
them to me, including the woman if she is one who
wishes to come. Seat the others under the shed near
the granary and have them covered by ten good riflemen
from the bunkhouse. They are not to know they are
watched. If there is any evidence of hostility, shoot
them all. Do not hesitate."

He took out a cigar, looked at it thoughtfully, and
added, "Better still, let Fraconi bring them to me. You
stay in command of the men in the bunkhouse. I trust
your judgement."

When Calder had gone he ordered coffee and sat
down in the hide chair with a book. It would be some
time before they arrived. He glanced around the room,
once more appraising his situation. He had guns placed
at various places through the room and was prepared
for any eventuality.

Kate Connery had no idea what would happen once
she reached the ranch of her uncle Martin. Her family
had not liked him, but on the one occasion she had
seen him he seemed romantic, adventurous, exciting.
She remembered him only as a very tall man, slender
and immaculately dressed.

The house was low, flat-roofed, and of plastered adobe.
On either side were rows of buildings. One was apparently a store-room; another might be a bunkhouse. The

barns and corrals were some distance away. There were hitching rails along both sides of the avenue leading to the house.

A stocky, powerful-looking man walked into the open space and stood waiting. As they rode up, he glanced at her, then at Ashford.

"There is something you wish?"

Ashford drew up. The man seemed to be alone, but he radiated strength and seemed in no way disturbed by confronting a column of armed men.

"I am Colonel Henry T. Ashford, of the Confederate Army. I wish to see Martin Connery."

"*Captain* Connery." Calder gestured toward the shed roof in front of what appeared to be a store-room. "You may leave your men there."

"I wish them with me."

Calder merely looked at him. "You will leave your men there. You may bring four people including yourself. If you do not like that, ride away."

Ashford was furious. Who was this man to speak so to him? Well, that could wait. After all, if he could get Connery's help it might save much travel and leave him a tower of strength when the ship arrived.

"Very well."

His men hesitated, then trooped toward the shade of the shed, tying their horses at the hitching rail.

Ashford turned in his saddle, looked around carefully, then dismounted. Only the one man in sight, but on a ranch of this size he would need many men. *Where were they?* He had an uncomfortable feeling they were not far off.

"Hayden, and Cutler. Come with me, please." He turned and looked at Kate. "You, also. We will hope for your sake that this uncle can help us."

"I did not promise that."

They walked over the hard-packed yellow earth to the steps, which led to the wide veranda that encircled the adobe house. Mounting the steps, they saw no one.

Cutler leaned close and whispered. "Colonel? We'd better be careful. I don't like this."

Ashford rapped on the door. After several minutes a slender Chinese appeared, dressed all in white except for a red sash.

"I am Colonel Henry T. Ashford. I wish to see Captain Connery."

"Show the gentlemen in, Lee."

The Chinese stepped back, and they walked into the coolness of a wide room, sparsely but elegantly furnished, totally unlike the cluttered parlors done in velvet and panels that Kate remembered.

Captain Martin Connery was standing. He was tall, as she remembered, with a lean face, high cheekbones, and a slender but powerful body. He must be, she thought, sixty years old. He did not look more than forty.

"Colonel Ashford?" He held out his hand to Cushing.

"*I* am Colonel Ashford!" Ashford said, irritated.

"Of course! How stupid of me!" Connery's face was bland. "Will you not sit down? You must have had a warm ride."

"Captain Connery, I will be brief. General Lee has surrendered. I have not. Some of us believe the Cause can still be won, and we go to Mexico to gather our forces, to recruit, to acquire weapons, and to prepare for our victorious march to the north."

He paused. "Your niece, Katherine Connery, was kind enough to offer to introduce me."

Connery smiled, holding out his hand. "It is good to see you again, Kate. I scarcely expected you to have a military escort."

"Colonel Ashford has also been kind enough to escort several young women, including one of the Traven girls. I believe he thought we would be in danger if left in our homes and would be much better off protected by his soldiers. In fact," her heart was pounding, "I believe he intends to protect us all the way into Mexico."

Ashford's features tightened with anger, but before he could speak, Connery said mildly, "You are perfectly welcome here, Kate." He turned to Ashford. "It would please me if you would bring the women here. They could remain here until it is safe for them to go home."

"They are with me. They will stay with me."

"Ah?" Connery was bland. "I do not quite understand what a southern *gentleman* has to do with carrying off women from their homes. In a military action women can be nothing but an encumbrance."

Ashford was coldly furious, but he fought down his anger. "It was not women I came to talk about. For the move I hope to make, I shall need horses to mount my men. I understood you had horses and believed you were loyal to the Cause."

"I see. And who is at the head of this move?"

"I am."

"Have you considered the logistics of such a move? Of the arms and ammunition you will have to obtain and to transport? Have you considered the feeding of an army of any size? I fear you are approaching this move with too little planning, Colonel.

"You will need not only your immediate supplies but continual replacements. You forget that was one problem the South had. Most of the munition factories were in the North. The South had the arsenals in the beginning but they did not have either the food or the munitions to continue such a struggle."

Colonel Ashford had been a volunteer, elected to

command by the men of his unit, as were many officers
of both the North and the South. As such, his experience with command was slight. He had been, until near
the end of the War, when he was leading what was
virtually a guerilla outfit, entirely dependent on the
supply system of the Confederate Army.

"We shall have no problem. We will live off the
country." Ashford was uneasy, wanting to avoid the
subject. Why had he come here in the beginning? This
man was not going to help. What they wanted they
would have to take.

"You amaze me," Connery was cool, smiling gently.
"You would live off the very people for whom you are
supposed to be fighting? I do not think they would
appreciate that, Colonel Ashford. I am afraid you'd
encounter much resistance. As far as that is concerned,
I doubt if there is ammunition enough in all east Texas
to fight one major battle. You are dreaming, sir."

Ashford placed his hand on his pistol. "No more of
this!" he said sharply. "You have horses, you have
supplies. We need them. If you will not volunteer
them, we shall take them!"

THIRTEEN

Connery took up his cigar and placed it in his teeth. He was smiling. "I think not, Colonel." He spoke quietly. "And do not try to draw that pistol. Blood discolors my floor. Right behind you gentlemen is Carlo Fraconi. He has held a gun to you, Colonel, for several minutes."

"My men are outside," Ashford said, "within a minute I could . . ."

"I am afraid, Colonel, that you continually over-estimate your situation. Your men are neatly arranged under the shed in front of my supply room. Opposite them are some of my men, one of them covering each one of yours. If a shot is fired in here, your men will be wiped out on the instant."

Martin Connery drew gently on his cigar. "I would suggest you retire from the scene, Colonel. Take your little army and ride away."

"Kate," he said, "you may remain here until such time as I can send you safely home, with an escort."

"I can't, Uncle Martin. I have to go back to those other girls. They need me."

"Ashford, I want you to free those girls. Free them at once."

"Go to Hell!" Ashford was shaking with fury. "You have the upper hand now, but wait! Just wait!"

"Shall I kill him, Captain?" Fraconi asked.

"No, please!" Kate exclaimed. "Please, don't! He is the only protection those girls have! Please don't kill him!"

"Very well." Connery dusted ash from his cigar. "You may go, Ashford, but if any harm comes to those girls or to Kate Connery I will personally see you skinned alive. And I mean just that. Now get out! Get off my place! And stay off!"

As they reached the door he said, "My advice would be to free those women at once. We in Texas do not take kindly to men who abuse women."

Fraconi watched them go, saying, "You could have held some of them hostage."

"No, Carlo, for he would have sacrificed his men. Don't you see? He's completely without honor or loyalty. Whatever veneer there was on the surface has peeled off during the War. He is a man without a code, without a sense of honor. Probably he deluded himself that he was an officer and a gentleman. Underneath that facade he is neither."

"What will we do?"

"I want you to go into the woods and find the Travens. They are woodsmen, I understand, and they are very careful men, so be alert. Perhaps together we can do something."

When Fraconi was gone Connery walked to the side-board and poured a drink. He had acquired a taste for rum, and although he often drank it was always sparingly. He had the feeling that whatever situation arose he could cope with it if sober, so he never intended to be otherwise.

There was every chance that Ashford would attempt to drive off some stock from his ranch or one of the others nearby.

Except . . . suppose there was a ship coming? Suppose he took the girls off to sea?

Out there on Mission Bay he had his own ship, a fast vessel with eight guns, and he kept it ready for sea at all times. After all, a man needed a way out.

He was here, he had come to love the ranch, and he had no plans to leave, but just in case, the schooner lay waiting. He called it, after the vessel in an old sea ballad, the *Golden Vanity*. There was no vessel in the American seas that could out-sail or out-maneuver her.

If Ashford took the girls to sea, he would take in his anchor and let out some sail, and he could lay alongside of whatever ship they had within hours.

Ashford led the way back to their horses. Mounting without a word, he rode toward the gate. The others followed, walking their horses.

Kate held back, riding behind Ashford, unwilling to risk what might follow and feeling his shame.

Martin Connery had made him out to be a fool, had shamed him before his own men, shown them he was inadequate. As she rode she was thinking ahead. The story of what happened inside would get around. One of those who was there would talk, and Ashford would lose control.

For one wild, desperate moment she wished she had

stayed behind, for when Ashford lost control the men
he had commanded would become a rabble. The first
thing on their minds would be the girls in that wagon.

She had to get them away. They must escape. Nor
could there be any delay. She would have to chance it
at the first opportunity and just hope they could meet
the Traven boys.

Suddenly their pace was too slow. She had to get
back. What could have happened while she was gone?
Just suppose . . .

She did not want to suppose. She wanted only to be
back, to see the girls again, to plan.

Somehow they had to get away, and they had to get
away now. She could already see the men hanging
back, and Cutler and Hayden were whispering among
themselves. And once, looking back, she caught their
eyes on her. Suppose, just suppose, one of them decided to pull away from Ashford now?

At the first sign of trouble she was going to use her
spurs. She was going to get out of there.

They were coming up to the shores of Mission Bay,
ready to cut out around it. Suddenly, glancing off toward the Gulf, she saw a ship!

Quickly, she glanced at the men. Hayden and Cutler
were hanging back, deep in a whispered argument of
some kind. Cushing rode somewhat abreast of her, yet
closer behind Ashford. They had not seen the masts.
Only topm'sts showed through the trees, still some
distance off.

Quickly, she averted her eyes, praying they would
not see it. Now she knew. She had to get away. She
must get to the girls and get them away at once! At the
very first opportunity, or even without opportunity,
they must go!

Where was Dal? And Mac? Where were they *now*?

Inside she was so frightened she was almost ready to cry. There were still several miles to go and they were *walking* their horses!

Desperately she fought to keep her composure, to keep her face from showing her fear and her worry. If only . . .

Mac Traven was waiting no longer. Bellied down in the sand at the edge of the forest, the Travens had been watching the wagons. With Ashford gone discipline had relaxed. Two of the men were down at the edge of the water, fishing. One stood on a rock, casting out into the water and slowly drawing his line in toward him. Two others were asleep under the supply wagon.

Others were lying about the fire or talking. "Jack," Mac suggested. "You an' Jesse can't run as fast as us. You be ready to cover us. We're goin' in."

"How you goin' to get away with that many women?" Jack protested. "It ain't sensible!"

"I've a hunch our time is up. We've got to do it now, before the others get back. If shooting starts, shoot to kill. We've no choice, and that's a lot of thieves and murderers out there."

He waited, using his field glasses. Suddenly, his eyes caught something. He lifted the glasses a little higher.

The topmasts of a ship!

Silently, he passed the glasses to Dal, then to Jack and Jesse. Now there was no question. They had to make their move.

"Wait a minute," Dal suggested. From an inside pocket he took a small hand-mirror. Glancing at the sun, he tilted the mirror to catch the sunlight, directing it into the wagon through the opening, praying one of the girls would see it.

Almost at once Mrs. Atherton got out of the wagon. He gave one quick flash into her eyes, then into the wagon again. One by one the girls got out.

They were close enough so that in the still air her voice carried. "I'll make some coffee. Dulcie, you and Gretchen gather some wood."

"There's a sharp woman," Jack said. "I'd hang up my hat for a woman like that!"

The girls walked toward the woods, stopping to pick up sticks. Nobody seemed to pay any attention. Then one of the men under the wagons sat up, wrapping his arms around his knees, he was watching.

Mac put away his glasses and put a reassuring hand on his belt gun, then passed it to Jesse. "You can use this," he said. "Remember, get the girls away."

The other girls had scattered out, picking up sticks.

The man under the wagon who had been watching crawled out. "You've got enough. Come on back!"

"You want to get wood for tonight?" Dulcie asked. "If we do it you don't have to, and I'm tired of settin' in that ol' wagon!"

One of the other men sat up. "Maybe she's lookin' for a walk in the woods, Charlie? Why'n't you see?"

"Hell, the Colonel will come back. He'd raise Hell."

"Suppose he does? I'm gettin' tired of just layin' around when we got all those women. I think . . ."

He started to get up, and Dulcie paused. "Just you set still! I'll be back." She walked into the woods as if going for a reason and Gretchen followed.

When Dulcie was still ten yards from the woods she saw Jesse. "Come on," he said, low-voiced, "this is the time."

"Hey, you! Come back here!"

One of the girls suddenly panicked and started to run. A man lunged up from under a wagon, smashing his head against the under-pinning. Swearing bitterly, he held his head in both hands.

The man who had first shouted at Dulcie now started after her, running. Happy Jack let him come. "This one's mine," he said. When the man was almost ready to reach out and grab Dulcie, Jack said, "Over here, Mister!"

His voice was low and could not be heard beyond where the man skated to a sudden stop. He looked at Jack and he went for his gun. Jack fired and the man doubled over, and suddenly men were leaping up from all over.

Mac Traven held his Spencer .52 in his hands, and he watched the girls coming, running toward him. Men started up, and several started coming toward them. Jack's shot brought them to a sudden stop as they realized there was more involved than just the girls.

Mac threw his rifle to his shoulder and shot a man in the rear who was turning toward a wagon, obviously to pick up his rifle. Then coolly and taking his time, he shot three more without changing position.

"Jesse!" Dal shouted. "Gather the girls an' get 'em away! Back to our last hide-out!"

Dal was firing steadily, then reloading his pistol with an extra loaded cylinder he carried.

Mac waved him back. "Let's get back into the woods!" Firing was general now. "Jack! Get the horses!"

Mac moved along the edge of the woods. The fishing men had disappeared. Caught on the open beach, virtually without cover, they ducked and ran for any shelter they could find, dropping behind hummocks of sand, the wheels of the wagons, or anything else.

Yet there were perhaps a dozen of them left, and some were skilled fighting men. Without direction they broke into a rough skirmish line and started for the trees.

Happy Jack waited, studying the situation. The horses were in a rope corral running from one of the wagons, around a stunted pine, then on to the supply wagon and back to the first wagon. When all eyes were on the woods he stepped out quickly and knife in hand, slashed the rope. Instantly, he grabbed the nearest horse and riding Indian fashion drove the rest of them ahead of him into the trees, whoopping and yelling.

Dal caught a horse and Jesse another. Mac retreated, pausing to slip one of the loaded tubes from his Blakeslee Quick-Loader into the butt of the Spencer in place of the empty.

Ducking swiftly among the trees and herding several horses before him, he headed for their last hide-out. It was a matter of seconds now. They had to get the girls mounted and out of here before the attackers closed in.

There would be no quarter now, for anyone. They would be killed on sight and the girls taken where they happened to be caught.

Mac turned, facing toward the woods, backing swiftly away.

What about Kate? Where was Kate? What would happen to her?

FOURTEEN

Kate's horse, feeling her excitement, had edged a little ahead, and they were almost to the small stream they must cross that emptied from a lake into Mission Bay. Beyond were some trees. Suddenly, ahead of them, there was an outburst of firing.

Instantly, she pointed out across Mission Bay toward the wider waters of Copano Bay. *"Look!"* she cried.

Ashford turned his head, saw the masts and sails of a ship, heard the firing, and was distracted only an instant. Kate leaped her horse into the stream, crossed it quickly, and turning at right angles, slapped the spurs to the horse and raced for the woods.

A rifle came up. *"No! No!* Take her alive! Don't shoot!"

Cushing grabbed his sleeve. *"Colonel! The camp! We're attacked!"*

"It's the Travens! Go in fast and we'll get 'em!"

They went over the beach and up to the wagons at a dead run. The horses were gone, four dead men lay on the ground and three others wounded, one of them moaning for help. From inside the woods they heard an occasional shot.

Ashford pulled up at the wagons. "Cushing, see what you can do for that man. Hayden, Cutler . . . try to catch up some of the horses. They've been stampeded."

A glance into the girls' wagon told him they were gone. Well, they wouldn't get far. He had too many men.

They started for the woods, and he ordered them back. "There's enough out there now. Get some coffee, get something to eat. If they come up empty you're going to have to go out."

Butler came toward him, explaining. "Came right out of nowhere, Colonel. Sudden attack. Some of the boys were fishing, an' . . ."

"I left you in command, Butler. I depended on you."

"Yes, sir. I am sorry, sir, but I was having trouble with some of the men. They wanted the girls."

Kate . . . that damned Kate! He should never have trusted her, not for a minute. Yet he had not trusted her, just been a little careless.

He got down from his horse and looked around with a sudden feeling of emptiness, of loss. It was not Kate. It was simply that everything was getting away from him, and that damned Connery had seen it. Who was he to be so sure of himself? What had he ever done?

One of the soldiers had pulled a log up alongside the fire, and Ashford went now and sat down. He took his hat off and ran his fingers through his thinning hair. What had ever possessed him to kidnap those women, anyway? Nothing but trouble and more trouble. Trouble with his men, bringing the Travens down on him, and giving Connery the opportunity to make a fool of him.

He had to think . . . think! He had the hat, and there was a rabbit in there somewhere, if he could just lay hold of it. Somehow he could bring victory from . . . he started to say defeat but shied from the word. He could yet win. He had to win.

Butler came up to him with a cup of coffee. "Here, sir. You're tired, sir, and you haven't eaten."

He accepted the coffee. "Thanks, Butler, you're a good man."

Butler turned sharply away and stood for a moment. No, damn it, Butler thought, he was not a good man! A loyal man, maybe, but nobody in this outfit was a *good* man.

He had been a good soldier. He had fought hard, but when the Confederacy lost, he lost, and he should have gone home like the others instead of following this wild-goose chase. Again, it was that sense of loyalty carried too far that had brought him here. Being loyal was not enough. One had to be loyal to the right cause, the right person. How many men and women, Butler wondered, had been trapped into trouble and even crime out of a sense of loyalty?

Or was it an unwillingness to recognize evil in one's friends?

He remembered once when he was a boy he and several other boys had been egged on by the one who was their leader into abusing a smaller boy. He hadn't wanted to but lacked the courage to say no. Was it the same now?

Butler walked away toward the sea, watching the ship, which had grown large on the bay as it drew nearer. What kind of a man was he, anyway?

What had happened down there at Connery's ranch?

Whatever it was it had shaken Ashford, and they had obviously been unsuccessful. Cushing would tell him, if he asked.

Was he going to ask? After all, what difference did it make? This was over, anyway. They had played out their string and there was nothing left.

A horse . . . what he needed was a horse.

Two miles back from the coast Mac and Dal Traven rode up to where Happy Jack and Jesse had stopped with the girls. "Move out," Mac said. "Don't wait a minute longer. Right over there is Refugio. You know it, Jack. Take the girls there and find shelter for them, a home or a hotel, somebody who will put them up."

"What about you?"

"Dal an' me have got to find Kate. She's out here somewhere. That outfit's going to Hell in a hand-basket. They're falling apart, and as they do, they'll get meaner.

"Don't waste time, Jack. There's the Mission River. Don't try to follow it—it's too crooked. But if you keep it in sight it will take you right to Refugio."

"You don't need to tell me. I know Refugio."

Mac turned sharply. "Jack? You haven't been in trouble there, have you? I mean you can go into town?"

"You make it sound like a feller's been in trouble wherever he goes. No such thing. I got friends in Refugio, and it's a right nice little place."

When they were gone, Dal turned toward his horse. He stopped beside it, sat on a log, and began to clean his pistol. "Kate's a good woman, Mac. She's the best."

"You get that gun ready, Dal, and we'll go find her."

He sat down on a log and leaned his head back. If he could sleep! Just for a minute . . .

* * *

Kate Connery had skirted some marshy ground and found herself pushed further north and a bit west. She walked her horse into the woods, looking for a place to hide. She was sure they would come looking for her, but . . . shots, a lot of shooting off toward the wagons.

Finding a small knoll she rode up it, and from among the trees she could look off in the direction from which she had come. She was in time to see the last of the detachment racing off toward the fighting.

So she was alone. Yet could she be sure? They might have sent somebody after her.

She got down and led her horse into the deepest, darkest patch of woods.

What now? The Travens were out there now, and one of them was Dal. When she had believed Dal was dead she had turned away from all men for over a year, then Frank Kenzie, who was a good, decent man, had started coming around, hat in hand, to see her. She liked him. He was nothing like Dal, neither as exciting nor as strong, but what was a girl to do? Dal was dead. At least, she had believed he was dead.

Sort of.

She could never quite believe it, and that was why she had shied from actually marrying Frank. Now Dal was back, and she might have lost him. By this time he would know about Frank.

The distant shooting ended, and there was only silence.

What should she do? Standing beside her horse, she tried to picture the situation. Shooting at the wagons could only mean the Travens had made an attack or attempted one. To go there now would mean she would be riding right into trouble. The Travens would have

their hands full, and there was no way she could help.
If she only had a gun!

Like many another western woman she had been
shooting since childhood and had often hunted so her
family could eat. There had been no convenient stores
where food could be bought. Out where she lived
people grew their own corn, ground their own flour,
made their own molasses, and gathered from the forest,
as had the Indians. Several times she had helped to
defend their cabin against Indian attacks.

Yet she had no weapon. Dal had always said that if
somebody wanted to kill a person lack of a gun would
never stop him. There were too many other weapons
just lying around a house or barn.

Looking around she found a stick, not over three feet
long. It was part of a broken branch, and she stripped
away the smaller twigs. She liked the feel of it in her
hands. At least, she felt better.

What *had* happened? She was restless and worried,
and never one to stand still. She had always done
things, not waited for others.

Think . . . what could have happened? The Travens
had made an effort to rescue the girls. That was more
than likely. They had succeeded or they had failed.
They might have been killed. On the other hand, they
might have escaped.

Suppose they got the girls away from Ashford. What
then? Neither Mac nor Dal was apt to keep the girls in
the woods, where an attack might recapture them. So
they would send them away to a safer place.

Refugio or Victoria, and Refugio was closer. Who
would go with them? Jesse was still not quite recovered
from his wound, so it would be him.

If they got the girls safely away with either Jesse or

Happy Jack guarding them, Dal and Mac would come looking for her.

The girls would have told Dal that she had gone off to the Connery ranch with Colonel Ashford. At the fight near the wagons, Ashford and some of his men had come racing in, but where would they think she was? They had two alternatives. She had either been killed or left at the ranch. There was a third, of course, which was the actual one. She had escaped.

The renegades would come looking for the Travens and for her also. And the Travens would be looking for her.

They would ride south toward Mission Bay, and she must try to intercept them.

This was the land formerly held by the cannibalistic Karankawa Indians, and deep within the forest one might still find remains of ancient fires, and sometimes bones, but they had been primarily fish-eaters.

The forest itself covered thousands of acres of mixed growth, scarred by long-ago fires. Closer to the beach the trees grew more stunted, and there was piled-up debris left from bygone storms that had broken over St. Joseph's Island and the peninsulas to wreak havoc on the inner shores.

Trees blown down by hurricane winds or destroyed by insects lay scattered about everywhere through the undergrowth. There were few tall trees, most of what was there being trees of medium height mixed with brush. Here and there were small groves of pecans.

Kate Connery was restless. It disturbed her that she did not know what was happening, and she had never been one to sit and wait.

Also, she was too close to where she had disappeared. If anybody came seeking her, this was where they would start. She started off, leading her horse.

At first she was only weaving her way among the trees, finding ways to get through, avoiding obstructions and seeking a trail. She found one.

It was a game trail, obviously used by larger game but showing no indications of recent travel. She mounted her horse and still holding her stick, followed the trail, which led north and then west. Nowhere did she see any tracks.

It was very still. Occasionally, she drew up to listen but heard nothing.

A soft wind from off the Gulf stirred the leaves, causing faint rustlings that worried her and caused her to stop and listen again and again. A branch or a piece of rotting bark fell from a tree and she came up standing, listening, frightened.

Once, near a rotting log, she glimpsed a huge old diamond-back rattler, thicker than her arm. Her horse shied, but she was a good fifteen feet away and not worried. Yet its presence was a warning. There could be others.

It was very still. Twice she saw great white birds sweep by overhead, whooping cranes. There were numerous tracks—a small black bear, many raccoons, even an alligator.

She drew up again, listening. Something moving. Something large, therefore something or someone who might be dangerous. She put her hand on her horse's neck and spoke softly to it, sshing it.

She heard the sound again. Something . . . not very far off. Something moving.

She let her breath out carefully. How far away? Was there more than one of whatever it was?

What could she do? *Run?* But from what? From whom? It could be an enemy. It could also be one of the Travens or one of the girls.

She gripped her stick a little tighter. What was it Dal had said? *Thrust, don't strike*. Instinct seemed to make one wish to use a stick as a club, but the thrust was better, at the throat, the face, the mid-section. Jab with it and jab hard, or grip the stick in both hands and jerk it up under the chin . . . *hard*.

Movement, not very far off. Suddenly, bitten by a fly, her horse stamped a hoof. Movements ceased.

"Over there," a man said.

Not one of the Travens, yet a familiar voice, not one pleasantly familiar, either. Her mouth was dry and she tried to swallow, tried several times before succeeding. She gathered the reins, hesitating. Exactly where *were* they?

There was movement, she glimpsed a horse's head, then the rider. Behind him, another rider.

"Well, would you lookit this! An' all alone, too! Just you an' me an' the lady, Cut. Jus' the three of us. I'd say we were gonna have us a time!"

Cutler and Hayden, and she was alone. . . .

FIFTEEN

She slapped the spurs to her horse and went down the trail as if shot from a gun. Ducking her head because of low branches she raced down the narrow trail, and seeing another turning off to the north, she whipped into it. Her horse leaped a small stream and ducked under a low-hanging limb.

They were close behind and coming fast. If only she had a gun! The trees arched over the trail, and at places wind had bent them down until they almost closed the trail. Running wasn't going to be enough. She'd have to fight. They were too close behind, and the first time she encountered a real obstruction her horse would stop and they would close behind her.

What would she do? Stab for the face with the end of the stick, then take off again.

Kate was angry. She did not like to run, and she despised the two men who were pursuing her. Yet she was no match for them in any kind of physical encounter, except briefly. Well, make it brief then!

Suddenly there was a log across the trail. How good a jumper was her horse? She did not know, but she headed him right at the log, and he went for it, sailing right over it in a long, graceful leap. She pulled up quickly as Hayden's horse balked, and turning in her saddle she struck him across the face with her stick.

His hand had gone up to block the blow, but too slowly. Her move had been unexpected and swift. Her stick smashed Hayden across the face, and then she was gone again, racing away down the winding trail.

Coming suddenly into a small clearing with a fallen-in cabin, she turned at right angles and raced off down a road of two ruts with grass growing between them. Her horse seemed happy to run, and she gave him his head. A glance back showed they were coming.

Rounding a bend in the road she saw before her a low hanging branch. She ducked . . . too late!

She hit the ground hard, and her horse went racing off. She heard a yell of triumph, and Hayden hit the ground as she came up. His face was bloody, and there was an ugly welt where she had struck him. It looked also as if his nose might be broken. That she glimpsed in one startled moment as he lunged to grab her.

She jerked the stick up, gripping it with both hands, and as he lunged at her she ripped the jagged end of the stick into his throat, just back of the chin.

Hayden gave a strangled cry and fell back, blood gushing from his throat. Cutler dropped from his horse and rushed at her.

She backed off a little, choosing her ground. "Come on!" she invited. "You can have what he got!"

Cutler was wary. He circled.

Hayden was on his hands and knees, choking on his own blood. "Heh . . . help me!" he pleaded.

Cutler ignored him, circling, watching her like a cat. "You throw down that stick!" he said. "You an' me, we can git along. We don't need him. We don't need nobody. Jus' you an' me?"

"You'd better take care of your friend," Kate said calmly. "I'm not afraid of you, and the Travens are coming. They're bringing the rope to hang you with!"

Cutler was a heavy, powerful man, but quick. She must be very, very careful! What was it Dal always said? "You got to think of the terrain. You got to use the ground."

The place where they were was a clearing in the forest not more than fifty feet across, edged on one side by a marsh with no water visible, its surface covered with a thick mat of water lilies and clumps of sedge. As a child she had often hopped from one such clump of sedge to another, but the water-lillies in between often grew over deep water.

There were some scattered pines, much undergrowth, and other trees. She backed off, toward the edge of the lilies, and Cutler followed, his eyes on her.

How much did he know? Of how much was he aware? To make her first leap she must turn her back on him, something she was loathe to do, yet suddenly, she did just that. She turned and leaped for the nearest clumb of sedge, feeling his hands grasping, slipping off her arms as she barely eluded him.

She landed on the sedge, sagged dangerously but came erect and leaped to the next clump. Unaware he lunged after her and ran right into the lily pads. He went down, came floundering to the surface gasping. "Damn you! I'll—"

Coolly, she leaped to another clump of sedge, then

running to the nearest horse she caught up the reins and got into the saddle.

He was floundering in the water and lily pads. "Help me! Help! *I can't swim!*"

"Everybody has troubles!" she said, and rode away.

It was Cutler's horse, and there was a rifle in the scabbard and a pistol in a saddle holster.

She was armed. Now she could look for Dal.

Dal holstered his gun and looked over at Mac. "Well, boy, this is what it all comes to. You and me and them. If we don't get out of this alive I just want to say no better man ever lived, and I've been proud to have you for a brother and a friend."

"That goes double, Dal, but you and me, we can make it. We've got to for Kate's sake, and then we've got to take the girls home.

"You know, Dal, I wonder what happens to men like Ashford? He was a respected man, and he could have gone on to make something of himself. Now he's thrown it all away."

"He was rotten at the core, Mac, like one of those pretty red apples a man bites into sometimes. What it all comes down to in the end is a matter of honor and simple decency. If a man doesn't have that, he's nothing, and never will be anything, no matter how many cows he owns."

"You ready?"

"If I ain't I never will be. We got it to do, boy, and I've a hunch here's where the shootin' starts."

Mac stepped into the saddle and edged ahead of Dal. He was thinking, Dal had Kate if they could find her, and who did he have?

He had known a lot of girls, but when it came down

to now, where were they? And who would shed a tear if he folded his cards on this trip? Just nobody, outside of his family.

Sunlight filtered through the leaves and dappled the grassy trails. Shadows lurked deep under the trees in this scattered, stunted forest. He saw the tracks where several javelinas had crossed the trail, leaving the deep, sharp little prints of their passing. They didn't leave much of a mark, but who did?

He drew the Spencer from the scabbard. A pistol was all right, but for a man with strong hands a rifle was better. He could shoot straighter, farther, and harder, and he had learned to shoot a rifle like a pistol, shooting right from where it was.

"Must be twenty of them left," Dal said. "Maybe even more."

"Makes it about even," Mac said, grinning at him over his shoulder. "But let's you an' me find Kate and dust out of here. They don't have anything we want."

"Yes, they do. Back yonder in that wagon they've got coffee, bacon, and . . ."

"Ssh!" Mac lifted a hand, and they reined in, listening. They had come close to the edge of the woods, and they could hear the sound of a ship's bell. Edging forward, from a low sand-hill they could see a ship at anchor on the bay, a boat being lowered into the water.

"We weren't any too quick, Dal," Mac said.

"I hope to God nothing keeps them from getting to Refugio! After all this . . ."

"They'll make it."

"There's Ashford, going out to meet them." Mac got out the field glasses. "Butler's with him. Must be him, from Jesse's description, and there's a half dozen others."

"Anybody at the wagons?"

"Are you thinking what I think you are?"

"Well, look at it. Kate's out there somewhere needin' help, but she'll also be hungry, and it won't do no good if we starve. Besides, I think we should send up a signal."

"There'd be ammunition, too, and I'm down to one more load for my pistol."

They turned their mounts and rode back into the trees, keeping back from the edge of the forest. After all, the two groups approaching each other would be watching each other, not the wagons.

There were many tracks, but they had been ridden over too many times to identify. When they were within fifty yards of the wagons they pulled up. "Nobody in sight," Mac whispered.

"Let's go."

They walked their horses out to the wagons. "Get what we need, Dal. I'll stand watch."

Only a moment or two passed, and Dal emerged with a sack of coffee and a slab of bacon. He returned for some jerked beef, a loaf of bread, and a sack of lead bullets.

"Get me some powder, too."

"Make it quick."

"Hold your horses. I've found me one o' them Quick-Loaders. I just want to make sure she's all loaded up."

He disappeared. Mac was sweating. He mopped the sweat from his eyes with his sleeve, looking all around. The two groups had come together on the sand near the sea. They were talking now.

"Hurry, Dal!"

Dal was climbing out of the wagon when the three riders came out of the brush. They were riding toward the wagons when Mac saw them, and a moment later they saw him. For a moment they stared, then rifles came up, and Mac shot the Spencer from where it was and saw a man fall. He rode his horse away from the wagons to draw fire from Dal and shot again. The man's horse leaped, throwing him off balance and momentarily out of the fight.

Mac spurred his horse, leaping him toward the third man and they fired simultaneously. Mac felt something snatch at his collar, and his shot missed. His second, fired at a dead run toward the third man, did not.

Wheeling his horse Mac charged at the last man, who was fighting his horse into control. As he came up to the rider he lifted his rifle for a point-blank shot when the man jerked and fell sideways off his horse.

Dal came up as his shot sounded in their ears. "Don't be greedy," he said.

At a dead run they rode into the woods. Dal pulled up at the narrowing trail. "You hurt?"

"No . . . but it was close."

"Closer than you think. You've got blood on your collar."

Mac put his hand up, touching his neck gingerly. A graze. A half inch further over and he might have bought it. Now the sweat was getting into the wound, and it stung. He took out a handkerchief and made a square of it and tucked it between his collar and the wound.

"Anyway," Dal said, "we won't starve, and I'm loaded for bear. I got one of those six-cylinder Quick-Loaders. Maybe we should start this war all over again."

"You start it. When we find Kate, I'm going home. At least," Mac added, "I'm going back where we came from."

They rode again into the woods, weaving their way deeper and deeper, then turning south again.

Mac was tired, and he knew Dal was. They had been riding and fighting . . . how long since they had slept?

Or eaten? Yet they could not think of that now. Kate was out there, perhaps in dire need.

"Hell of it is," Dal said, "we don't know what she's riding, if she is riding anything. We don't even know what to look for."

It was hot. Dal mopped the sweat from his face and looked around. So much of this wooded place looked like any other. They pushed on.

Something over an hour later they rode into a grassy clearing to see a standing horse and a man sprawled on the ground.

Mac stepped down from his horse and turned the body over with his boot toe. The man's nose had been broken. There was an ugly welt on his cheekbone and the skin was split, but his throat had been pierced and torn.

"What in God's world?" Mac said. "Would you look at that!"

"Kate," Dal said.

"*Kate?* Are you crazy?"

"No, sir. Kate, with the end of a stick. I showed her how. Don't you remember what we learned from that character named Dugan? To thrust with a stick, not strike?"

Mac stared at the body. "Dal, take some advice from your big brother. If you marry that girl, be nice to her. You hear me?"

SIXTEEN

Night was coming, and Kate was alone. The big horse she was riding was fractious and difficult. She was tired and wanted to rest. Twice she had riders pass within a few yards of her, but now they seemed to be riding back toward the beach. From a word or two she had overheard she was sure the ship she had glimpsed was now at anchor.

If so, Ashford would be meeting with them, but what did he now have to offer? Perhaps there was money in one of the wagons; she did not know. She knew of none in her wagon, but she had heard of secret compartments in the floors of such wagons.

Now she wanted, desperately, to rest. She was hungry, but it was sleep she needed most. But *where*? How? There must be two dozen men roaming through the woods aside from the Travens. From time to time she heard outbursts of firing.

Suppose she rode to Connery's ranch? To do so meant she must ride across open range for some distance, and in clear view of anybody who was watching. The big horse she rode was tired and could not stand a long run.

She had seen nothing of the girls, although a glimpse of the wagons indicated no movement, not even guards, hence nothing to guard. They had been taken away or had escaped.

Martin Connery had offered to let her stay, but she had chosen to return to help the girls. They had needed her, but now they were gone. Where, she did not know.

There was a small chain of lakes that ran parallel to Mission River. So far there had been no movement or action there, and if she could find her way she might find a place where she could simply lie down, if only for a few minutes.

She had checked the rifle and pistol she had acquired along with the horse. Both were loaded, both ready for use. Yet she had only the ammunition they carried, no more.

Stopping by a small stream she let the big horse drink, and lying down, she drank from the stream near her horse, holding the reins.

It was a quiet place. She looked around a small clearing, then went back to the edge of the trees, leading the horse.

There was a place there under the trees, a mossy green place. There was a rope on the horse, and she picketed him on the grass, tying the rope to the tree near her. Putting the rifle on some leaves at her side, she slid the pistol back under the leaves but where it could be quickly reached. Only then did she lie down. Almost at once, she was asleep.

Darkness gathered in the forest, and stillness was its companion. Small animals began to prowl, and in the trees birds ruffled their feathers. An owl questioned the darkness, then flew past on silent wings, a ghostly predator sweeping through the trees. A red wolf, seeking prey, smelled the sleeping girl, the horse, the sweaty leather of the saddle, and shied away, interested but wary. A snake crawled by within a few feet, but the horse snorted and stomped his feet, and the snake moved away, headed toward the nearby lake and the frogs it heard.

Bats swirled and dived and fluttered in the starlit darkness above the stunted forest. The sleeping girl turned on her side, and the rider heard the movement and drew up to listen. He heard the horse cropping grass, then slowly and carefully dismounted. The leather creaked as he swung down, and for a moment he stood very still, afraid the sound had awakened her. After a moment he tied his horse to a tree.

Tip-toeing to make no sound he went near her, looked down at her for a moment, then crossed to a nearby tree and sat down where he could watch her. He took off his wide sombrero and laid it, crown down, on the grass. After a moment he took off his boots and placed them carefully alongside his hat. Then he drew a pistol and laid it in his lap.

The girl turned restlessly in her sleep, and his hand went to the pistol, but she relaxed into deeper sleep.

In the deep stillness of the night a great flock of the whooping cranes swept in to a landing on the lake, settling like a white cloud upon the dark water. For a long moment the lake and the forest were silent, then slowly the night sounds renewed their strength.

In the last hour before dawn frail streamers of mist

floated in from the sea, huddling among the trees like so many ghosts called to picnic upon the damp grass. The man with the pistol returned it to his holster and shaking out his boots, drew them carefully on. Then he tip-toed to his horse and returned with a coffee-pot. He dipped water from the stream where a spring bubbled beneath the surface, and gathering dry wood from underneath old logs or breaking tiny twigs from the trunks of trees, he put together a small fire.

A thin tendril of fire lifted its questioning smoke, and the man selected a larger bit of dry wood from near a lady-slipper. The man looked at it. "You are the tricky one," he whispered. "You are the deadly one."

He walked back to his fire and added wood to boil the water. "Beautiful," he whispered, "and deadly." He glanced at the sleeping girl. "She is the same, I think."

When the water was boiling he added coffee and went back to sit by his tree.

Kate Connery opened her eyes to a gray sky above a canopy of leaves. Streamers of light touched the wraiths of fog, and they shuddered like virgins approached by lechers and disappeared. The sunlight remained. The girl lay still, not quite awake, not quite free from dreaming, only slightly aware of the coffee smell.

She sat up abruptly, and the man smiled and doffed his hat. "Buenos dias, señorita. I am Fraconi."

"I remember you."

Her rifle was still beside her. To place the situation in proper perspective, she drew her pistol from under the leaves and placed it in her lap.

He smiled. "Coffee will soon be ready. The bacon, I regret, must be grilled over the fire. It will lose something, yet when one is hungry . . .?"

"I will enjoy it."

He got to his feet in one swift, graceful movement. "There . . ." he pointed, "is a sheltered place where this stream enters the lake. If you wish to bathe or wash your face and hands, it is yours." He smiled again. "I regret the amenities are less than I would wish."

"You work for Captain Connery?"

He smiled again, a very different smile. "We are associated. Occasionally he has things for me to do. I do them. Otherwise, I am indolent. I live upon his bounty, on his ranch. I have fine horses to ride, enough to eat, occasionally a bottle of wine. Such a life is very simple, señorita. I prefer it so."

"He is near?"

"He is on the ranch, I believe. With Captain Connery one is never sure. He shares his decisions with no one. He might be there, he might be here. He sent me to find the Travens. Instead I have found you, which is better."

Kate went into the trees and looked back. Fraconi was at the fire, his back to her. She bathed a little, splashing water on her face and shoulders. Then she put on her blouse and returned to the fire.

"Eat," he suggested. "There may be much riding."

She accepted the cup he offered and took bacon from the pronged stick hanging above the fire. She had not realized she was so hungry.

"You are an interesting woman," he said.

She looked at him coolly, not sure what was in his mind. "Each in his own way may be interesting," she said.

"You would kill a man, I think."

"If it were necessary. One does what one must. One survives," she added.

"Back there," he waved a hand at the woods, "I

found a dead man. His throat was badly torn. I think he choked on his own blood."

She felt a little sick, and said nothing. "One dead man," he added, "but two hats. One floating on the water."

"Everybody," she said, "should learn to swim."

He cut strips from a slab of bacon and hung more on the prongs.

"I am no longer hungry," she said.

"Eat!" he commanded. "We have much riding, and we do not know when we will eat again. Drink much coffee . . . it will help."

He walked away from the fire to listen. When he came back he said, "They are moving again, gathering on the beach, I think."

"But you cannot see them?"

"Of course not. They are far away. Nevertheless, I think that is what they do, and I think the Travens look for you.

"Last night I tell myself this. I look for the Travens. They look for you. So if I wait with you, they will find you, and I shall find them. So, it is simple, is it not?

"Besides," he added, smiling, "it saves much riding, much looking, much trouble. I am, as I have said, indolent."

She looked at him over her coffee-cup. "I do not think you are indolent. I also think you are a gentleman."

For the first time he looked slightly embarrassed. "I am complimented."

He sat silent for a few minutes, and then he said, "It is good of you to say so, but in all honesty I must confess I am something of a rascal, and Captain Connery knows it well."

"And yet he has you working for him?"

He looked up, some pride in his words. "He trusts me, señorita."

"You are not Spanish?"

"Italian, but I grew to manhood in Spain and in the Canary Islands."

He saddled the horses and led them to water. Kate waited, listening for some sound from the forest or the beach. It was such a relatively small area, and yet with so many enemies about neither those who looked for her nor she herself dared attract attention, for fear it would be the attention of the wrong people.

She had for what seemed a long time lived only from hour to hour, even minute to minute, so that she longed for home—her own kitchen, her own yard, her own people. And Dal was out there, perhaps wounded and dying.

Fraconi lingered. "I would take you to Captain Connery despite the fact that he sent me for the Travens, but we should go after dark when we can cross the open plains without being seen. Those salt grass meadows offer no cover except here and there a low spot."

"I want to find the Travens. I believe we should look because if we do not they will continue to look for me, risking their lives all the while."

They rode out, toward the beach.

The wagons remained where they were, but there were neither horses nor oxen near them, and the beach itself was white and empty. Drawn up on the beach were three boats, but there was not a man in sight, not any movement.

Puzzled, Kate stood in her stirrups . . . nothing. Fraconi looked equally puzzled. "Three boats? Each, I think, will carry twenty men, although I doubt they carried so many. Yet how many? And where are they?"

There was a stirring behind them. Fraconi turned like a cat . . . too late.

There were a dozen men there, seamen by the look of them. All had guns. The man in command was a surly-looking ruffian. "Lift no hand if you wish to live," he said, "and get down from those horses!"

Kate slapped her heels into her mount and as the horse leaped forward she dropped to the far side of him, Indian-fashion. The horse leaped into a run and was plunging for the sand-hills when a shot rang out, then another.

She felt the horse shudder as he took the bullet, but as he started to fall, she sprang free. She had not grown up on a ranch for nothing.

She sprang free, tumbled upon the sand, and got up and started to run.

Then they were all around her, and two men grabbed her arms, jerking her roughly around.

"Do her no harm," the officer said, "that was most expressly mentioned. She's worth a thousand in gold if she's unharmed."

He glanced at her appraisingly. "I'd give two thousand, myself!"

He glanced around suddenly. "Damn it all! Where's the other one?"

Fraconi was gone.

He swore bitterly. "Did none of you see him?"

"It was her we were sent to get, sir," a seaman said. "When she tried to get away, we tried to stop her."

The officer shrugged. "Very well, forget him. He was of no importance, anyway. Take her now. She goes aboard ship."

Then he lifted his hand. "Hold up! We must let Captain Hammond know, and Colonel Ashford as well.

Jamie," he said to the boy with them, "run off for the Captain now. Do you be telling them we've captured our prize. We will wait here."

The boy ran off, and there was silence. The officer glanced at the men. "You may smoke," he said, "but be watchful. She's a tricky lass."

"And a niece to Captain Martin Connery," she said.

There was an absolute silence, then the officer said, "What was that you said, ma'am?"

"I said I was a niece to Captain Connery, whose ship the *Golden Vanity* lies in Mission Bay, if you will but look."

She'd heard it said that seamen knew of each other as landsmen often do and that reputations travel far. It had been said that seamen, wherever they might be, knew of Martin Connery and his ship.

"Mr. Masters, sir?" He was a tall young man with blond hair. "We didn't reckon on this, sir."

"And neither did I," Masters said irritably. He glanced at Kate again. "Ma'am? You are niece to Captain Connery, of the *Vanity*?"

"I am, and was with him only two days ago or so. The man who escaped works for him. By now he will be well on his way, and he can be," Kate lied, "at his home within the hour."

If a fast horse would not get her away a fast tongue might. "The *Vanity*," she said, "has eight guns and a Long Tom . . .," she had that from a story she'd read, "and he can be at sea in a matter of minutes."

Masters swore bitterly. "What's your name?" he demanded.

"Kate . . . Katherine Connery."

Masters swore. The men were uneasy, glancing around, then toward the sea.

He turned to her. "Did Colonel Ashford know who you were?"

"He knew, but he is not a man of the sea. So he knew yet he did not know."

Masters paced, swearing softly, bitterly. "Will that boy only *hurry*?"

SEVENTEEN

Sometimes a half-truth is better than none. When one deals with the enemy one uses what tactics one may, and she was not being actually dishonest. She simply said, "Captain Connery said anyone who bothered me he would personally see skinned alive."

"He'd do it, too!" the blond man exclaimed.

"He knows you are here?"

"I rode back with Colonel Ashford to see the other girls freed; then they took me prisoner."

"What of the others?"

"They are gone, taken off to Refugio, and by now the people there know what is going on. There should be a posse leaving Refugio by now," she added.

Masters swore again, and the blond man said, "Mr. Masters, sir? Running guns is one thing, even slaving, but who wants to challenge Martin Connery? Who, sir?"

"Be still!"

The morning wore on, and there was still no word from the forest. Masters sat on the sand, paced, swore, and looked off to sea.

Masters was wishing he was back aboard ship and standing out to sea. Whenever he got off a ship's deck he got himself in trouble. At sea he knew he was, as a seaman, one of the best. Ashore he always seemed to stumble into trouble. But no man in his right mind went cross-ways of Martin Connery, and there were stories by the dozen of men who for one reason or another tried to get the better of him. Not one of them was now afloat.

The blond man stood up. "They're coming, sir! The captain's coming back!"

"Thank God!" Masters said. At least, the burden of decision would no longer be his.

Hammond was a thick-set, heavy man who walked over the sand without effort. He glanced at his men, then at Kate.

"Captain, sir? This young woman is Kate *Connery*."

Hammond was irritated. "I am not interested in her name, Masters! As far as I am concerned she is a piece of merchandise. Very pretty merchandise, I might add."

"Sir, you did not hear me. She is Kate *Connery*, Captain Martin Connery's niece."

There was a moment of deadly silence—then Hammond turned on Ashford. "What kind of a trap is this, Colonel? I agreed on guns for women. Then it turns out you have only *one* woman, and now she turns out to be Captain Connery's niece!"

"I've seen Connery. There's nothing about him to be afraid of!"

"*You've* seen Connery? Like Hell, you have! The man's

a devil! Follow you to Hell an' gone if you cross him! Did you ever hear of the Dead Man's Chest, Colonel?"

"Something in an old sea ballad, isn't it?"

"It's that, and more. It's a rocky bit of island without water, without trees, without anything, and it sits right under a tropic sun!

"There were some men who believed themselves tough enough to challenge him, so he put them ashore on the Dead Man's Chest and left them there. Told them they'd soon discover just how tough they were, and he'd come back for them, sooner or later.

"He went back, all right, but there wasn't much left. What thirst and the sun hadn't done they had done to each other!

"There was another time a man tried to double-cross him and have him murdered into the bargain. It failed, an' Connery followed him to sea, put a couple of holes in his ship's hull, then took the crew off as she was sinking. When their captain, who'd tried to have Connery murdered, started to leave with them, he sent him back.

"'A captain is supposed to go down with his ship. Isn't that the tradition? Let's see you live up to it!' Then he sailed away."

Hammond turned away. "I've had my sail for nothing, Colonel Ashford, but never try to make any gun deals with me, or any kind of deals. Before you start stealing girls, you'd best find out who they are!"

The wind from off the sea had a taste of salt. Ashford stood, staring at the ship that was to have brought him arms. Over there on the shore, men were getting into boats. Others, who had been waiting in the sand-hills, followed.

Frank turned and walked to the wagon. Several others, guessing his purpose, followed. Ashford turned sharply. "Here, you! None of that!"

Frank stopped, spat, and said, "Go to the devil!" And walked on.

Kate stood very still. There was a horse over there, bridle reins trailing. She started toward it, walking slowly.

"Kate! Where are you going?"

"I'm going home, Colonel."

"You're leaving me, too?"

"I was never with you, Colonel. It looks to me like you'd better find yourself another world. You will get no credit in this one."

She walked on.

"Kate! Stop!"

Several of the men, scattered out en route to the wagon and its whiskey, stopped. Kate kept walking. Only a few steps more. Just a few steps . . .

"Kate, damn it, I said *stop!*"

She had almost reached the horse. Just another step or two, and once in the saddle, she would . . .

"I'll make her stop, Colonel." It was Frank. Suddenly he lifted his rifle and shot the horse dead.

Frank lowered his rifle, then reached in the back of the supply wagon and took out a bottle. He tossed it to the man nearest him, then another to the next man. He took a bottle for himself, and then they started walking toward Kate.

She turned to face them. There was no place to run to, just nowhere to go.

"Dal," she said aloud. "Dal, where are you?"

Without turning her eyes from the advancing men, still some fifty yards off, she said to Ashford, "Toss me your pistol!"

"What?"

"Toss it to me or use it! If you won't stop them, I will!"

He hesitated, then suddenly drawing a pistol he tossed it to her. She caught it deftly.

The men stopped, irresolute. She stood quietly, facing them, waiting.

"Go ahead," one of them said. "She won't shoot nobody!"

"Where's Hayden?" she asked them suddenly. "What became of Cutler?"

"Come on, she won't shoot! Let's go get her!"

"You go," one of them backed off, pulling the cork from his bottle. "I helped bury Hayden!"

He took a drink and wiped the back of his hand across his mouth. "Go ahead, Frank! You started this. Let's see you handle her."

Frank started forward, then stopped. He stopped and slowly began to back away. One by one the others did likewise.

Kate held the gun steady, never taking her eyes from them. "It's all right now, Kate." The voice was Dal's. "Just mount up an' we'll get out of here."

For a moment her relief was so great she thought she would faint right away. Her knees were suddenly weak, and slowly she lowered the pistol. Then without looking at Dal or Mac, she walked to her horse, gathered the reins, grasped the pommel, and putting a toe in the stirrup, hesitated.

They had found her. She was free. The other girls were free. It was over . . . almost over. She swung into the saddle.

Only then did she trust herself to look at them. They were there, Dal with his pistol and Mac a little to one side with that Spencer rifle he carried.

She walked her horse over to Ashford and handed

him the pistol. "Thanks, for that much." She reined her horse around. "If I were you I'd get out of here while the getting is good. When they have a few more drinks they are going to get mad, and you got them into this."

"I'll manage."

She walked her horse to where Dal waited, and he spoke softly. "This ain't over yet. Just walk your horse off an' be ready to make a run for it. We'll hold 'em until you get out of range."

"I want to be with you."

"You are with me. Now get goin'. I been to a lot of trouble to find you again, and I don't figure to get you shot."

Frank tilted the bottle. He was watching the Travens. To Hell with this! Ashford might let her get away, but he wasn't going to. Just wait, he told himself, I'll take some of those high an' mighty airs away from her. Before I'm through she'll set up an' beg!

Nevertheless, he waited, taking another drink. "This ain't over," he said to the man, Bolt, who stood near him, "not by a long shot!"

"Be careful! Those boys can shoot!"

"How many horses we got?"

"Ten, twelve maybe. What about the Colonel?"

"He's washed out. There's nothing to him."

Ashford stood alone on the white sand. He was empty. He looked off toward the bay, seeing the ship lying there. They were getting sail on her, heaving up the anchor. Soon they would be standing out to sea . . . it was over, over.

He looked around to see Butler and Cushing walking over to him. "Colonel? I believe we should get out of here. Ransdale is holding horses for us over by that live oak. I think we should ride back to Kentucky."

Kentucky? He had never amounted to anything in

Kentucky, and he would be nothing now. He felt sapped, drained of energy. "I don't know, Butler. I just don't know."

"Sir? There isn't much time. Some of those men have a real hate for you. Some are just renegades, prepared for anything. They are a rabble, sir."

"But they are our rabble."

"Not any more, sir. Come, we must go now. We're attracting too much attention."

Butler glanced toward the wagons, then turned away, Cushing walking beside him. After a moment of hesitation, Ashford followed.

Mac Traven let Dal and Kate ride away while he sat his horse watching. When they were a good two hundred yards off, he turned his horse and followed, riding rapidly to catch up, but he did not turn his back on the wagons.

When he topped a rise four hundred yards away, he pulled up and looked back. Three men, one of them Ashford, were walking away. A number of the others were grouped around the wagons.

"Dal, I want to go home!"

"We're goin', Kate, but we'll stop in Refugio long enough to pick up the girls an' Mrs. Atherton. There'll be some time in Refugio for some other business, too."

"What business?" she asked suspiciously.

"You an' me gettin' married, Kate. I come near losing you one time, and I don't want to risk it again."

"I suppose I should consider that a proposal?"

"I reckon it could stand for one. I never was very handy with words, and since I got wounded the first time I've had a stiff knee. If I got down you might have to help me up. There's still a bullet in there somewhere. Doc said he'd cause more trouble gettin' it out than the bullet would if it stayed."

Mac rode up beside them. He glanced back again. He was not at all sure they were free and clear. That was a bad outfit, and some of them were very tough men. After a moment, he fell back again. Dal and Kate were talking, oblivious to all but themselves, and he needed to listen.

If there was an attempt to follow them the pursuers would probably ride right for Refugio by the most direct route, while Mac had already decided to stay south of Mission River until he reached the main road into Refugio.

Nor must they linger in Refugio, but leave at once for Victoria.

The day was bright and clear. From the higher ground they could catch an occasional glimpse of the bay, and the ship could be seen approaching the passage into Aransas Bay. Mac took off his hat and mopped his brow. He was beginning to feel the let-down after an action, and it was too soon.

Home! Now he could go home. He could work around the place, repairing the pole corral, leaks in the shed roof, the doors and windows on the house. He wanted nothing so much as to be back doing the simple, everyday things.

He wanted to be riding the range again, branding the stock long left unbranded due to the War.

He turned again in his saddle . . . nothing.

Why should he feel so uneasy? What was wrong? Yet the feeling persisted.

Dust . . . he smelled dust! He called out. "Dal! Somebody's coming! Look alive now!"

Horsemen were coming, at least twenty of them, and seven or eight of them Indians. They drew up. Mac

Traven pushed a little ahead, his Spencer across the saddle in front of him.

There was a tall man in a Mexican sombrero and a dozen very tough, capable-looking white men, Anglos or Mexican.

The tall man whipped off his sombrero and bowed. "Kate? Are you all right? These, I take it, are the Travens?"

"That's right," Dal said, "and who are you?"

The man smiled. "I am Martin Connery. Occasionally called Captain Martin Connery." He glanced at Kate. "You are all right? And the other girls? Are they also all right?"

"Everything is fine now. Dal Traven, Martin Connery. Dal and I are to be married." She turned in the saddle. "Major Mac Traven."

"The pleasure is mine. We were coming to see if all was well, and also, well, we here in Texas like to keep our beaches clean. We thought we might ride down and clean things up a bit. Odds and ends, you know."

"Some of those odds and ends," Dal said, "are drinking the whiskey they found in the supply wagon. I believe Ashford has gone off with a couple of the others."

"We shall see, shan't we?" Connery raised his hat again. "Hasta la vista!"

EIGHTEEN

Happy Jack walked across the plaza to greet them as they rode in to Refugio. He was smiling. "Mac! Dal! Sure good to see you! I was figurin' you got chewed up down there an' I was goin' to have to come down an' pull you out from under those fellers!"

He held out a hand to Kate. "Good to see you, ma'am, I guess you folks been through it, but from what those girls tell me they'd never have made it but for you."

Mac glanced around the square. People were watching them, and these were good people. He wanted to visit no trouble upon them. "Are they rested? Can they travel?"

"They're itchin' for it, but how about you folks? You must have been goin' day an' night?"

"We'll make it. I'd like to go on to Victoria."

Dal protested. "Kate an' me, well, we . . ."

"You can be married in Victoria just as well as here, maybe better. There's a lot of good German folk there, and they like marriages and such. Let's get out of here."

When Kate had gone off to see the girls, Dal said, "Mac? What's bitin' you? That's all over. Those folks are whipped, and when Connery gets through with them there won't be enough left to hide under your hat."

"Maybe. I say we get out of here, get some distance behind us. Some of those boys got away, and I don't know what Ashford's got in mind."

He tied his horse to the hitching-rail and went into the hotel. In Jesse's room he bathed and shaved, then trimmed his mustache. Happy Jack came in with fresh clothes. "Found a store open. You get shined up now." He paused. "You sure you want to start tonight?"

"No," Mac hesitated, "I guess not. It will give all of us some rest, which we can use. Anyway, I don't want to be on that road at night with all those girls. Get Dal an' me a room, Jack, and we'll bed down here for the night."

"Where are the girls?" Dal asked.

"Cottage down the street. Mrs. Atherton's with 'em, and I been sort of watchin' around, too."

"I'll just bet you have!" Dal said dryly. "I've seen you watchin' around ever since you first saw Mrs. Atherton."

"Somebody's got to look out for 'em." Jack was embarrassed. "Anyway, she's a widow lady. You told me so yourself."

It was a pleasant town, and people went about their business, only partly aware of what had been happening only a few miles away. Mac cleaned and reloaded his guns, checked the tubes in the Quick-Loader, then stretched out on the bed.

"You boys rest," Jack said. "Me an' Jesse will keep a

tight rein on things tonight. Besides, I've had me a talk with the marshal, an' he's put an extry man on, just as precaution. These are good folks, and they don't trifle around much."

In the small hotel things were quiet. From time to time people walked along the hallways, and there were subdued voices from the various rooms. Yet for all his weariness, Mac had a hard time falling asleep. For four years now he had slept with an awareness that he might have to rise at any moment.

"Four years?" he spoke aloud. "It's almost nine, if I count the Rangers, although there was a good night's sleep there, time to time."

Outside the cottage where the girls slept, Happy Jack tipped his chair back against the wall and got out a cigar. He struck a match, revealing a face seamed by sun and wind, and eyes alive as a boy's yet wise with years. His eyes swept the square, seeing nothing. This was an early-to-bed town, except around the saloons, but even they were quiet tonight. A few late drinkers or poker players were active, but Jack had no desire to join them.

"There's somethin' to be said," he had told Jesse, "for just restin', for just settin' an' watchin' the world go by."

"Aw, now, Jack!" Jesse protested. "There's mighty little of it ever got past you."

"Well, a man has to get around some." He changed the subject. "Mac was sayin' folks back east killed off almost all their cattle durin' the war, and now they're short of eatin' meat. I been figurin' on tryin' a drive, maybe a thousand head."

"How will you get across the Mississippi?"

"Swim it. How else? Hell, Jesse, some of those longhorns would swim the Atlantic if they knowed there was grass on the other side."

"If you or Mac decide to try it," Jesse said, "you can count me in. Only I'm not swimmin' no river that size. I'll let you an' the longhorns do it. When I cross a river that big I'll be in a boat."

One by one the lights went out, and the square lay silent, the last dust settling, the last creaks going out of the boards. A lone dog trotted up the street, headed home from somewhere, and a cat crouched near the water trough in silent patience. Often in the late hours rats came to drink or to hunt for scraps of food dropped by passersby.

Wind rustled the leaves, and Happy Jack's lids grew heavy. The lone dog, sensing his presence, came up on the walk under the porch and sniffed at Jack.

"Set down, boy. You wasn't goin' nowhere you just had to be, now was you? Set down, an' we'll enjoy the night together."

He scratched the dog's ears, and the dog lay down, watching the cat. He had chased that cat before, and twice was more than enough. He had learned about cats.

The bartender came to the door of the saloon and threw a bucket of dirty water into the street, glancing over where Happy Jack sat. Wise in the ways of trouble, he had seen them all come and go, lumberjacks, track-workers, cattle-drovers, cowboys, sailors, river-rats. Every wrinkle or line on Happy Jack's face he could match with another, for the years had marked his cheeks with experience, with laughter, with tears, with anger and with sadness, until there was left only a vast patience.

He would have liked to walk over and sit on the stoop with Jack, not necessarily to talk, just to sit there and share the night and the years with him. They had been through it, even if not together. The bartender remembered how it had been from the Bowery to Charleston to Mobile and New Orleans, and how it had been in Cincinnati and Louisville and St. Louis and even Frisco. He walked back inside and took off his apron, then blew out the last light and crossed the floor in the dimness to enter his own small room at the back.

People often asked him why he did not marry, but he had been married twice and all that his wives had done was spend his money and complain about his hours, and he could do that for himself. It was a matter of quiet pride that he always poured an honest drink and never short-changed a drunk. He liked to talk a little with a few chosen people, but he never gambled. He had watched it too long from behind the bar, and he had known too many short-card experts and their like. He had put aside a little for the future, but it had all come from honest earnings, and that was how he wanted it. His name was George Hall, and they called him Jersey George. He had a brother named Sam whom he had not seen for years and hoped he would never see again.

When his cigar was down to a stub Jack opened his eyes and rubbed it out on the board at his feet, then ground the end of it under his toe. A man couldn't be too careful about fire. These towns were mostly built from plank, and they'd go up like a tumbleweed if you touched a match to them. Along the street at intervals there were barrels of water for fighting fire, just in case. Behind one of those barrels, across the square, a man was crouching. The old dog pricked up his ears, scenting for indications.

"I seen him, old fella. You jus' set quiet now an' let him do his nosin' around. No use shootin' him. I'd just wake up all these nice folks."

Reassured, the dog stretched his nose out on his paws, but he kept his eyes on the shadowy, distant figure behind the barrel.

Happy Jack dozed a little, but his eyes caught the movement when the man left, and his ears caught the pound of racing hoofs in the distance. The man had left his horse on the edge of town, and the pound of those hoofs was a far-off thing.

"Damn fool," Jack told himself. "Why, I bet half the men in town heard him leave. Nobody runs a horse at this hour unless he's up to something."

Lying on his back in his bed the bartender heard it and knew that the kind of man who would go running from a place in the night without due cause was the kind who would never learn. He wouldn't live long enough. If he made that mistake, he would make others.

The rider reached the fire on Mission Creek. "It's all quiet," he said. "Nobody around but one of them Travens. The old one. He's settin' on the porch, sleepin'."

"He won't be asleep," Bolt said. "He's one of them ol' Injun fighters."

"We'll wait until they are on the trail," Frank said. "Buck, you're good with a rope? D' you reckon you could take one o' them out of the saddle without him yellin'? I mean, he'd be the last one in line?"

"It's a chancy thing but I'd say I could."

A man sleeping by the fire sat up suddenly, looking around. "Where's the others? Haven't they come in yet?"

There was a long silence, and irritably, he looked around. "Didn't you hear me? Where are they?"

"They won't be comin', Hob. We left there just in time."

"What's that mean?"

"That Connery feller? The one they said used to be a pirate? Seems he didn't like folks messing with his niece, so he rode up from his ranch and he found the boys at the wagon, just stirrin' around, I guess."

Hob stared. "So?"

"He hung 'em. All four. He hung two of them to a tree and the other two to propped-up wagon tongues."

Hob stared from one to the other, prepared to believe they were joking. Finally he said, "Just like that?"

"It's like those fellers on the ship said. He doesn't waste around."

"I don't, either!" Frank said.

"We'll hit that bunch when they're all strung out. There'll be three, four of them, but there will be nine of us."

Nobody said anything, so he added, "We'll have all those women, we'll have their horses, whatever money they are holdin', and their guns. Then we'll just take out for the west. I got me a cousin over on the Neuces who is makin' a fortune stealin' cattle on both sides of the border. We can join up with him or start our own outfit."

Back in town Jesse came around the corner of the cottage. "All right, time for a change. You go rest those gray hairs."

Happy Jack stretched. "There was a fella lookin' us over from behind the barrel. I reckon that's all he was doin', but none of that bunch have much sense, so keep your eyes open."

Morning came with a low gray sky and a slight wind

blowing in from the sea. Before the sun was fairly in the sky they had moved out upon the road, with Dal leading off.

As they were mounting up, Mrs. Atherton went inside the hotel. The old man who ran it was standing behind the counter watching them. "I am Mrs. Atherton," she said. "I have no money with me, but I have a small ranch near the Trinity. I would like to buy a gun."

The cool old eyes regarded her thoughtfully. "Looks to me like you've got about all the protection you need."

"They are good men. The very best men, but one does not know what will happen. If I have a gun it might make all the difference."

"Can you use a gun?"

"I can. My father rode with Rip Ford and Jack Hays. He taught me."

"That's good enough for me." He reached under the counter. "This here's a gambler's gun. Deringer, they call it. And this here shoots just two bullets. You got to be fairly close to be sure of scorin', but I reckon if you have to shoot, that will be it. You can pay me when you're of a mind to."

"Thank you, sir."

Dal led off at a good fast trot and held it for the first quarter mile, then eased up, glancing back to let the thin column close up.

Kate rode up beside him. "You're worried," she said. "Something's bothering you."

"Look, I'm not going to be happy until we get you back where you came from. That bunch of renegades are trouble, lots of trouble.

"Most of them are gone . . . scattered! I don't know what happened to Ashford. He rode off with two or three of his friends, but he's a bitter man. His plans all went awry, and we're to blame.

"The rest of that lot are scattered around, none of them far from here, and they're all full of meanness and looking for a way to get even. So keep your eyes open. Anything can happen, and if it happens it will be between here and Victoria!"

"How far is it?"

"It would be a rough guess. I'd say forty miles, and we're goin' all the way through, no matter what!"

Kate turned and looked back at the thin line of the girls, Jesse, Happy Jack, and bringing up the rear, always in the place of danger, Mac.

She felt a sudden shudder of fear. They were . . . she *knew* they were near.

And tomorrow was to be her wedding day!

NINETEEN

It was a lovely, gently rolling land. Along the occasional streams were giant oaks and pecans, and upon the country around were clumps of mesquite and huisache with still a few of the golden blossoms. The season had been late. Daisies were scattered among them, often in great blankets of color. A few lingering blue-bonnets added their color.

Mac turned in his saddle and looked back, then let his eyes sweep the country on both sides, hesitating at anything unusual.

He was tired. It seemed he was always tired these days, and the sun was already warm. He pushed ahead, trying to close up the long column. It was spreading out too far as some of the horses wanted to lag. He pushed the last riders forward, urging them to keep the line closed up.

Again he glanced around. The country seemed virtually without cover, but he was too old a campaigner to believe that. There were always places a man could hide. If you didn't believe that, fight the Apaches.

Dal was almost a half mile ahead, much too far. "Jesse!" he called. "Close them up!"

Jesse was talking to Dulcie and only waved a hand, but he did begin to urge them forward. Slowly the gaps narrowed until the column was less than a quarter of a mile in length and slowly closing.

Dal pulled up on the crest of a hill, standing in his stirrups and looking all about. He should not do that. Made too good a target of himself.

They started on. Up ahead some trees came down close to the trail. A place to watch. Swiftly he swung out, cutting wide from the column and moving toward the trees. When he was nearer he got out his glass and studied them . . . nothing.

Nevertheless, he did not like the look of them or the rugged country around. Yet when they drew abreast of them, nothing happened. He scouted the near side, saw no tracks.

He squeezed his eyes together, then opened them wide. The easy gait and the hot sun were making him sleepy.

That Martin Connery now, there was a character! If he had been along with some of his men, especially that Fraconi, he'd have felt better.

The column was lengthening again, and he urged the laggards forward, growing irritated. Damn it, couldn't they realize the danger? A man would think that after what they had been through they'd be more cautious.

He topped a rise and went over it quickly, taking a look back as he did so.

He dried his palms on his shirt front, holding the

Spencer in his right hand, momentarily shifting it to the left.

He almost pulled up. As he shifted the rifle he thought he saw something ahead and off to the right. Must have been a flicker of light off the rifle barrel. Anyway, there was nothing there now.

Mac looked around quickly . . . nothing. Had he seen something or was it his eyes? He was very tired, and . . .

The loop came out of nowhere and dropped over his shoulders, totally unexpected. He was jerked from his horse, and the startled animal leaped forward and began to run.

He hit the road with a thump and heard a scramble of feet. When you roped something you hog-tied it. He knew that in a flash of realization and rolled over. He had clung to his rifle, and now as a man loomed over him he thrust the muzzle into the man's stomach and pulled the trigger.

In the instant before the gun went off he saw the startled look of awareness on the man's face. The instant that gun muzzle thrust into his stomach the man knew!

The blast of the gun knocked the man back, and Mac scrambled to his feet, trying to shake off the clinging rope before somebody else grabbed it.

The rope dropped free, and he glanced once at the man on the ground. He was dying and had no chance. The heavy .52-calibre slug had done its work.

He ran up the slope and saw the column scattered all over the plain. What seemed like a dozen or more men had charged down upon it, and with him knocked out of action their surprise was almost complete.

Jesse was firing, Dal had turned back, and several of the girls were bunching around Kate and Mrs. Atherton.

Mac dropped to one knee. The distance was well

over the two hundred yards his rifle was expected to shoot with accuracy, but he took careful aim, let his breath out slowly and squeezed off his shot.

A rider jerked in the saddle but continued to move. Taking his time, Mac fired again and again. Four shots. One man down, one man hit, and two clean misses!

A man on a blood bay horse was charging toward the girls, and Mac fired again. He evidently burned the horse, for it leaped aside, unseating its rider.

The fight was moving away from him. Quickly, Mac glanced around. Where was his horse? Where was the horse of the man who roped him? He saw neither, and took off running.

He could see it all up ahead. Then from the low ground before him a man raised up with a pistol . . . it was Happy Jack, and just as a rider charged down upon him, he fired.

The man went up in his stirrups, then fell, hitting the ground near Jack, who shot into him again. Scrambling, obviously wounded, Jack recovered the man's rifle and crawled toward the possible shelter of a place where run-off had scooped out the ground.

The fighting had gone over the rise in the ground and left him alone. He ran up to Jack. There was blood on his leg.

"I'm all right. I'm dug in an' I can handle myself. You get after 'em boy!"

On the rise before him there was a horse, reins trailing. He started for it, calling. It was his own horse. The animal hesitated, looking at him, but did not come. Slowly, he edged toward the horse and it moved away a little. He continued on, talking quietly. It was not a horse he'd had for long and although he moved hesitantly, it still shied away.

He gave up, dropping on one knee to survey the

field. Several men, a half dozen at least, were riding and shooting. The girls had bunched together but whether Kate was with them he could not see. He ran forward, carrying the rifle at port position, ready to fire on the instant.

Dal, on Bonnie Prince again, he could recognize at once. He saw Dal charge a man. They both fired, but Dal remained in the saddle. The other man dashed on by, and when at least fifty yards further on, he fell.

Mac took careful aim at a rider, led him a little and squeezed off his shot. The man left the saddle as if swept by a giant arm. The horse came racing on up the hill, and as he came abreast, Mac swung himself into the saddle and turned the horse back toward the fight.

His own horse followed, stirrups flopping at the gait.

The attack was broken. A few riders raced off, and he fired a futile following shot, then pulled up and reloaded. He walked his horse down the slope to the girls and saw Dal coming from the other side. He dropped the Spencer into its scabbard and looked around.

Jesse was coming toward them, limping. "Lost my horse," he said, "and a good horse, too."

Mac turned and rode toward his horse, which stood still, waiting. It was less nervous with a rider approaching than a man on foot. He caught up the bridle and rode toward Jesse. He swung down.

"Take this horse. I'll stick to my own." They both mounted. "Jesse, catch up a loose horse and take him down to Jack. Just over the rise."

Slowly, they gathered together. Jesse had been hurt when his horse fell, but aside from a bad bruise was all right. Happy Jack had a bullet through his leg. Neither Dal nor Mac had been hurt.

Gretchen had been grazed by a bullet that cut the skin on her shoulder. The others were unharmed, though very frightened.

Victoria was dark when they rode into town. Only a few lights glowed, one of them in what was called the Railroad Hotel.

Stiffly, Mac got down and walked into the lobby. A clerk with sleeve garters and a green eye-shade got up from behind a desk.

"If you got four or five rooms you could help us a lot."

"We've got the rooms, but I'm afraid there's no place for young women. I mean my rooms are partitioned off just with sheets of white cotton. No walls. Some of the men use some pretty bad language."

"You give us the rooms. I'll take care of the language."

He looked at Mac again. "Yes, sir," he said. "How many, sir?"

"Eleven beds. If you have two to a room, so much the better for some of them."

When they were shown to the rooms, Mac said, "We'll put the girls in the middle. Dal, you an' Jesse take the last room. Jack and I will take this one in front."

While they slowly filed into their rooms, Mac suddenly spoke out in his best parade-ground voice.

"Now *listen*! We've several very tired young ladies here. One of them is my sister. One of them is my brother's bride-to-be! I take it you are all gentlemen here! If you are, you will go to sleep and save the conversation until tomorrow. If you are not gentlemen I will personally attend to the noise-makers!"

There was silence. Then a voice said, "You just bed 'em down, Mister. We'll be quiet. Thank you for warning us. There isn't a man here who would use profanity in front of a lady!" Then more quietly, he said, "Now you boys shut up!"

There was a long silence, and then a voice said, "All right, Joe! We heard you! And we heard the gent who's with the ladies, so we'll shut up. But tomorrow morning when we see you in the street, you sure won't be no lady, and you'll get a cussin'!"

At three o'clock in the morning the town was dark and still. The man who dismounted at the corner of the hotel, tied his horse there, out of sight. He waited for a moment, listening, then came up on the board-walk. He peered into the hotel.

A light glowed over the desk, but nobody was in sight. Slipping off his boots he pushed a rawhide thong through two of the loops and slung them around his neck. Then he eased into the door.

Frank had made up his mind. The whole shooting match of a thing had gone down the drain. It was all over, but the one thing left to do. He was going to kill Mac Traven.

The lobby was empty but for some old newspapers scattered over a table and some chairs. A door was open behind the desk, and there was a bell on the desk to ring for the clerk, which would have been a futility, for all the rooms were gone.

Walking in his sock feet Frank went into the sleeping area, pausing suddenly, confused by all the ghostly white partitions. After the first moment, however, he realized it made his task the easier, for he could see through the cotton hangings. Although there was no light, there was a full moon outside, and Mac Traven's handle-bar mustache was like no other.

A gun or a knife?

A knife if possible. If not, a gun. In the confusion he could easily escape.

He was a burly, strongly built man, but he moved like a cat. That was Traven, right there at the end of the room, right where it would be easiest. Next to him two women were sleeping on low cots.

Those damn Travens! He never had liked them, seeing them around, riding their horses so big and brave! They'd never even known him, although before he joined up with Ashford he'd led a guerilla outfit that raided into Texas. Not that he led them. Guided was more what he'd done, although he could have led them, and better than he who did it.

He'd helped steal most of their horses and some of their cattle. He'd stolen Ranch Baby, the one they prized so much. He'd done it a-purpose, and it was Ranch Baby who was tied out there around the corner, waiting to carry him away after he killed Mac Traven.

He felt along the curtain, trying to find the opening that would let him through. He found the wrong one at first and stepped into the room where Dulcie slept in one bed and Mrs. Atherton in another. He stepped in ever so gently, but a board creaked and she opened her eyes. The moment they opened she was wide awake. She saw the man, saw that he clutched both a gun and a knife, but she had her Deringer.

Her eyes were on him, her hand moving ever so gently out from under the blanket. She held the gun out of sight below the edge of the bed, her thumb on the hammer.

The prowler was fumbling with the curtain. He was going into the compartment where Mac Traven lay. It was he whom the prowler intended to kill.

"Major Traven! Look *out!*"

The man turned like a cat, turned toward her, and she fired. The man jumped, then ran blindly at the curtain, hesitated there, torn between his desire to kill and the need to escape. Suddenly with a curse he tore down the curtain and ran for the door.

The cry awakened Mac and he came out of his bed, gun in hand. He saw the prowler and raced after him. The startled clerk lunged from his room in time to see a heavy-set man plunge through the outer door into the street.

Mac sprang after him, and the man turned sharply around, gun in hand. "Damn you, Traven!" The gun came up, and Mac Traven turned sharply, his right side to the man, and they both fired.

Mac saw the man shudder as he took the bullet; then he fired again.

Gun ready, he walked toward the man. He was on his knees now. It was the man called Frank. The man he had first seen in the streets of this very town. One of Ashford's men.

He was on his knees, his features twisted with hatred. "Damn you!" he muttered. "You've got all the luck! If it hadn't been for that woman . . . !"

Mac Traven waited, holding his gun ready.

The man was on his knees. He started to get up, then fell head-long. He lay sprawled on the board-walk, his fingers slowly relaxing his grip on the gun.

Lights were going on all over town. People would be asking questions, wondering, wishing these strangers would go away who had brought violence into their town. There hadn't been so much trouble around the country since the plague, and that was years ago.

Mac went back inside, glanced at the torn curtain, then looked over at Mrs. Atherton.

"Thanks, ma'am," he said softly.

ABOUT THE AUTHOR

LOUIS L'AMOUR, born Louis Dearborn L'Amour, is of French-Irish descent. Although Mr. L'Amour claims his writing began as a "spur-of-the-moment thing," prompted by friends who relished his verbal tales of the West, he comes by his talent honestly. A frontiersman by heritage (his grandfather was scalped by the Sioux), and a universal man by experience, Louis L'Amour lives the life of his fictional heroes. Since leaving his native Jamestown, North Dakota, at the age of fifteen, he's been a longshoreman, lumberjack, elephant handler, hay shocker, flume builder, fruit picker, and an officer on tank destroyers during World War II. And he's written four hundred short stories and over eighty books (including a volume of poetry).

Mr. L'Amour has lectured widely, traveled the West thoroughly, studied archaeology, compiled biographies of over one thousand Western gunfighters, and read prodigiously (his library holds more than twenty thousand volumes). And he's watched thirty-one of his westerns as movies. He's circled the world on a freighter, mined in the West, sailed a dhow on the Red Sea, been shipwrecked in the West Indies, and has been stranded in the Mojave Desert. He's won fifty-one of fifty-nine fights as a professional boxer and pinch-hit for Dorothy Kilgallen when she was on vacation from her column. Since 1816, thirty-three members of his family have been writers. And, he says, "I could sit in the middle of Sunset Boulevard and write with my typewriter on my knees; temperamental I am not."

Mr. L'Amour is re-creating an 1865 Western town, christened Shalaka, where the borders of Utah, Arizona, New Mexico, and Colorado meet. Historically authentic from whistle to well, when it is constructed, it will be a live, operating town, as well as a movie location and tourist attraction.

Mr. L'Amour now lives in Los Angeles with his wife Kathy and their two children, Beau and Angelique.

THE BUCKSKIN RUN BY LOUIS L'AMOUR

For the westerner, trouble came with the territory. Long grass valleys, merciless deserts, sheer rock cliffs, icy streams, hidden trails, dusty towns. These were the proving grounds of daily life. At any time violence could explode and on the frontier there was no avoiding its sudden, terrible impact. It was in these untamed places that men and women faced the daily challenge of survival ...

0 552 11910 5   95p

MILO TALON BY LOUIS L'AMOUR

To Milo Talon, there is nothing finer than drifting through the far, lonesome country. But times are lean, and when Talon hires himself out on a job, he finds himself suddenly hog-tied to a trail of trouble. He's hunting for the long-hidden secret to a fortune in gold. Along with a beautiful woman driven by a desperate fear, Talon is quickly caught in the gold-crazed treachery of liars, thieves and murderers tracking his every move ...

But when the fighting gets ugly, Talon's rule is plunge in and let the Devil count the dead!

0 552 11838 9   95p

THE MAN CALLED NOON BY LOUIS L'AMOUR

He came to in darkness, in a town he didn't know, with an aching wound in his head, his shirt soaked in blood – and an empty holster on his hip. He didn't remember what had happened – or who he was; not even his own name ... But one thing he did know, one thing that pounded along with the pain in his head: someone had tried to kill him, and would try again. For in the darkness he'd heard a whisper – 'Ben Janish swore he'd got him!' Not that time, but maybe the next time ...

0 552 09317 3   95p

YONDERING BY LOUIS L'AMOUR

Contains adventures of the sea, of war, of the exotic islands of the East, stories based upon experiences and people Louis L'Amour encountered during his early yondering days.

Most of the men and women of YONDERING do not face their challenge in the old West, yet they summon up courage and strengths that would have stood them well on the American frontier. They discover, as Louis L'Amour discovered in his own past, that in the daily act of survival, each of us conquers his own frontiers.

YONDERING, written with all of the sheer storytelling power that we have come to expect from Louis L'Amour, is a different and very special book.

0 552 11561 4   95p

COMSTOCK LODE BY LOUIS L'AMOUR

COMSTOCK LODE was just a godforsaken mountainside ... but no place on earth was richer in silver ...

They all came to the Comstock – drawn to its glittering promise of instant riches. Determined, they survived the brutal hardships of the mining camp to raise a legendary boom town.

But some sought more than wealth. Val Trevallion, a loner haunted by a violent past. Grita Redaway, a radiantly beautiful actress driven by an unfulfilled need. Two fiercely independent spirits, together they rose above the challenges of the Comstock to stake a bold claim on the future ...

0 552 11983 0   £1.75

THE BURNING HILLS BY LOUIS L'AMOUR

One against forty ... They had him cornered – up on a canyon rim with no way to go but down!

There was a rock big as a buckboard, right on the edge of the cliff. Trace bent, took hold and heaved. He felt his wound bust loose, but the rock rolled free. There was a rattle of stones behind it, then the echoing screams of a man and horse falling away into the darkness.

Bleeding and shaking, Trace yelled 'Come on, the rest of you, damn you!'

0 552 09352 1   95p

YOU'RE A TEXAS RANGER, ALVIN FOG

BY J. T. EDSON

In every democracy the laws for the protection of the innocent allows loopholes through which the guilty can slip ... The Governor of Texas decided that only unconventional methods could cope with the malefactors who slipped through the meshes of the law and so was formed a select group of Texas Rangers. Picked for their courage, honesty, and devotion to justice, they were known as Company Z ...

With one exception every man in Company Z had been a member of the Texas Rangers for several years. Alvin Fog was that man. He had inherited the muscle, skill at gun handling and bare handed fighting of his grandfather, the legendary Rio Hondo gun wizard, Dusty Fog. But still his fellows in Company Z were not convinced he had the skill needed for their unconventional duties. It was up to him to prove he was worthy of his place in Company Z. He alone could make his fellow rangers say ... 'You're a Texas Ranger, Alvin Fog ...'

0 552 11177 5   75p

McGRAW'S INHERITANCE BY J. T. EDSON

They were trying to cheat young Sandy McGraw. If it hadn't been for his friends they might have succeeded in depriving him of the ranch he had inherited.

But Sandy's friends were the right people to have on your side. One was Red Blaze, who always managed to find more than his fair share of any fights in his vicinity. Another was Betty Hardin, granddaughter of Ole Devil Hardin and an expert at ju-jitsu and karate. And the third was none other than the man with the fastest draw in the West, Dusty Fog.

Even so, the three friends found themselves in trouble over McGraw's Inheritance!

0 552 07900 6   95p

LOUIS L'AMOUR AND J. T. EDSON WESTERNS AVAILABLE FROM CORGI

WHILE EVERY EFFORT IS MADE TO KEEP PRICES LOW, IT IS SOMETIMES NECESSARY TO INCREASE PRICES AT SHORT NOTICE. CORGI BOOKS RESERVE THE RIGHT TO SHOW AND CHARGE NEW RETAIL PRICES ON COVERS WHICH MAY DIFFER FROM THOSE ADVERTISED IN THE TEXT OR ELSEWHERE.

THE PRICES SHOWN BELOW WERE CORRECT AT THE TIME OF GOING TO PRESS (FEBRUARY '83)

☐ 08131 0	**The Bloody Border**		£1.25
☐ 08133 7	**Wagons to Backsight**		£1.25
☐ 08134 5	**The Half Breed**		£1.25
☐ 08140 X	**The Peacemaker**		£1.25
☐ 12087 1	**White Indians**		£1.25
☐ 01307 6	**Comstock Lode (Large Format)**	*Louis L'Amour*	£2.95
☐ 11983 0	**Comstock Lode**		£1.75
☐ 11838 9	**Milo Talon**		95p
☐ 11910 5	**Buckskin Run**		95p
☐ 11561 4	**Yondering**		95p
☐ 11281 X	**The Strong Shall Live**		85p
☐ 10279 2	**Rider of the Lost Creek**		95p
☐ 10231 8	**Over on the Dry Side**		95p
☐ 09787 X	**War Party**		95p
☐ 09696 2	**Californios**		95p
☐ 09355 6	**Under the Sweetwater Rim**		95p
☐ 09352 1	**The Burning Hills**		95p
☐ 09351 3	**Conagher**		95p
☐ 09342 4	**Brionne**		95p
☐ 08673 8	**North to the Rails**		95p
☐ 08342 9	**The Silver Canyon**		95p
☐ 08157 4	**Fallon**		95p
☐ 07815 8	**Matagorda**		95p
☐ 08386 0	**Killoe**		95p
☐ 08341 0	**High Lonesome**		95p
☐ 09006 9	**Callaghen**		95p
☐ 09264 9	**The Ferguson Rifle**		95p
☐ 10357 8	**Where the Long Grass Blows**		95p
☐ 08939 7	**Tucker**		95p
☐ 09317 3	**A Man Called Noon**		95p
☐ 08574 X	**Flint**		95p
☐ 08388 7	**Kid Rodelo**		95p
☐ 08007 1	**Chancy**		95p
☐ 09387 4	**The Man from Skibereen**		95p
☐ 10639 9	**Borden Chantry**		95p
☐ 08486 7	**Taggart**		95p
☐ 08995 8	**Catlow**		95p
☐ 08642 8	**Reilly's Luck**		95p
☐ 10853 7	**The Mountain Valley War**		95p
☐ 10025 0	**Rivers West**		95p
☐ 09751 9	**Shalako**		95p

All these books are available at your bookshop or newsagent, or can be ordered direct from the publisher. Just tick the titles you want and fill in the form below.

CORGI BOOKS, Cash Sales Department, P.O. Box 11, Falmouth, Cornwall.

Please send cheque or postal order, no currency.

Please allow cost of book(s) plus the following for postage and packing:

U.K. CUSTOMERS. 45p for the first book, 20p for the second book and 14p for each additional book ordered, to a maximum charge of £1.63.

B.F.P.O. & EIRE. Please allow 45p for the first book, 20p for the second book plus 14p per copy for the next three books, thereafter 8p per book.

OVERSEAS CUSTOMERS. Please allow 75p for the first book plus 21p per copy for each additional book.

NAME (Block Letters) ....

ADDRESS ....

....